TIME WAS RUNNING OUT

Sadler knew that the discovery of heavy metals on the Moon could lead to a devastating war between Earth and the younger colonies of Mars and Venus. And someone in the quiet, respectable group of scientists on the Moon—someone Sadler had to find—was passing information to the unseen warships in outer space . . .

Was it Jamieson, the young astronomer devoted to the peaceful pursuit of pure science . . . or Jenkins, whose contacts in Supply gave him easy access to couriers from the rival planets . . . or even Director Maclaurin, whose knowledge of Earth's plans made him the most dangerous if he chose to tell . . .

If war came, the Moon would be the target. But Sadler's job was to prevent that war if he could . . . while the uneasy days, hours, seconds ticked away.

"AGAINST THE VIVID, UNBELIEVABLY REAL BACKGROUND OF LUNAR LIFE AND LANDSCAPE, CLARKE HAS TOLD A TALE OF ESPIONAGE AND COUNTER-ESPIONAGE, OF INTERPLANETARY POLITICS—A TALE, IN SHORT, OF SUPERSONICALLY HIGH-KEYED SUSPENSE!"
                                    —*THE NEW YORK TIMES*

Also by Arthur C. Clarke
published by Ballantine Books:

CHILDHOOD'S END
EXPEDITION TO EARTH
IMPERIAL EARTH
PRELUDE TO SPACE
REACH FOR TOMORROW
RENDEZVOUS WITH RAMA
TALES FROM THE "WHITE HART"

EARTHLIGHT

Arthur C. Clarke

A Del Rey Book

BALLANTINE BOOKS • NEW YORK

To
Dave Scott and Jim Irwin,
the first men to enter this land,
and to
Al Worden,
who watched over them from orbit.

A Del Rey Book
Published by Ballantine Books

Library of Congress Catalog Card Number: 55-6937

ISBN 0-345-27273-0

Manufactured in the United States of America

First Edition: February 1955
Eighteenth Printing: November 1977

First Canadian Printing: February 1958
Third Canadian Printing: October 1972

First *Bal-Hi* Printing: December 1965
Second *Bal-Hi* Printing: June 1966

Cover art by Stanislaw Fernandes

Chapter I

THE MONORAIL was losing speed as it climbed up out of the shadowed lowlands. At any moment now, thought Sadler, they would overtake the sun. The line of darkness moved so slowly here that, with a little effort, a man could keep abreast of it, could hold the sun balanced on the horizon until he had to pause for rest. Even then, it would slip so reluctantly from sight that more than an hour would pass before the last dazzling segment vanished below the edge of the Moon, and the long lunar night began.

He had been racing through that night, across the land that the first pioneers had opened up two centuries ago, at a steady and comfortable five hundred kilometers an hour. Apart from a bored conductor, who seemed to have nothing to do but produce cups of coffee on request, the only other occupants of the car were four astronomers from the Observatory. They had nodded affably enough when he came aboard, but had promptly lost themselves in a technical argument and had ignored Sadler ever since. He felt a little hurt by this neglect, then consoled himself with the thought that perhaps they took him for a seasoned resident, not a newcomer on his first assignment to the Moon.

The lights in the car made it impossible to see much of the darkened land through which they were racing in almost complete silence. "Darkened," of course, was only a relative term. It was true that the sun had gone, but not far from the zenith the Earth was approaching its first quarter. It would grow steadily until at lunar midnight, a week from now, it would be a blinding disk too bright for the unprotected eye to gaze upon.

Sadler left his seat and went forward, past the still-arguing astronomers, toward the curtained alcove at the front of the car. He was not yet accustomed to possessing only a sixth of his normal weight, and moved with exaggerated caution through the narrow corridor between the toilets and the little control room.

Now he could see properly. The observation windows were not as large as he would have liked; some safety regulation was responsible for that. But there was no internal light to distract his eyes, and at last he could enjoy the cold glory of this ancient, empty land.

Cold—yes, he could well believe that beyond these windows it was already two hundred degrees below zero, though the sun had sunk only a few hours before. Some quality of the light pouring down from the distant seas and clouds of Earth gave the impression. It was a light tinged with blues and greens, an arctic radiance that gave no atom of heat. And that, thought Sadler, was surely a paradox, for it came from a world of light and warmth.

Ahead of the speeding car, the single rail—supported by pillars uncomfortably far apart—arrowed into the east. Another paradox; this world was full of them. Why couldn't the sun set in the west, as it did on Earth? There must be some simple astronomical explanation, but for the moment Sadler could not decide what it was. Then he realized that, after all, such labels were purely arbitrary, and could easily get misplaced when a new world was mapped.

They were still rising slowly, and there was a cliff on the right which limited vision. On the left—let's see, that would be south, wouldn't it?—the broken land fell away in a series of layers as though a billion years ago the lava welling up from the Moon's molten heart had solidified in successive, weakening waves. It was a scene that chilled the soul, yet there were spots on Earth as bleak as this. The Badlands of Arizona were equally desolate; the upper slopes of Everest were far more hostile, for here at least was no eternal, ravening wind.

And then Sadler almost cried out aloud, for the cliff on the right came to a sudden end as if a monstrous chisel had sliced it off the surface of the Moon. It no longer barred his view: he could see clear round to the north. The unpremeditated artistry of Nature had produced an effect so breathtaking that it was hard to believe it was merely an accident of time and place.

2

There, marching across the sky in flaming glory, were the peaks of the Apennines, incandescent in the last rays of the hidden sun. The abrupt explosion of light left Sadler almost blinded; he shielded his eyes from the glare, and waited until he could safely face it again. When he looked once more, the transformation was complete. The stars, which until a moment ago had filled the sky, had vanished. His contracted pupils could no longer see them: even the glowing Earth now seemed no more than a feeble patch of greenish luminosity. The glare from the sunlit mountains, still a hundred kilometers away, had eclipsed all other sources of light.

The peaks floated in the sky, fantastic pyramids of flame. They seemed to have no more connection with the ground beneath them than do the clouds that gather above a sunset on Earth. The line of shadow was so sharp, the lower slopes of the mountains so lost in utter darkness, that only the burning summits had any real existence. It would be hours yet before the last of those proud peaks fell back into the shadow of the Moon and surrendered to the night.

The curtains behind Sadler parted; one of his fellow passengers came into the alcove and took up a position by the window. Sadler wondered whether to open the conversation. He still felt a little piqued at being so completely ignored. However, the problem in etiquette was solved for him.

"Worth coming from Earth to see, isn't it?" said a voice from the gloom at his side.

"It certainly is," Sadler replied. Then, trying to be blasé, he added: "But I suppose you get used to it in time."

There was a chuckle from the darkness.

"I wouldn't say that. Some things you never get used to, however long you live here. Just got in?"

"Yes. Landed last night in the *Tycho Brahe*. Haven't had time to see much yet."

In unconscious mimicry, Sadler found himself using the clipped sentences of his companion. He wondered if everyone on the Moon talked like this. Perhaps they thought it saved air.

"Going to work at the Observatory?"

"In a way, though I won't be on the permanent staff. I'm an accountant. Doing a cost-analysis of your operations."

3

This produced a thoughtful silence, which was finally broken by: "Rude of me—should have introduced myself. Robert Molton. Head of Spectroscopy. Nice to have someone around who can tell us how to do our income tax."

"I was afraid that would come up," said Sadler dryly. "My name's Bertram Sadler; I'm from the Audit Bureau."

"Humph. Think we're wasting money here?"

"That's for someone else to decide. I've only got to find *how* you spend it, not why."

"Well, you're going to have some fun. Everyone here can make out a good case for spending twice as much money as they get. And I'd like to know how the devil you'll put a price tag on pure scientific research."

Sadler had been wondering that for some time, but thought it best not to attempt any further explanations. His story had been accepted without question; if he tried to make it more convincing, he would give himself away. He was not a good liar, though he hoped to improve with practice.

In any case, what he had told Molton was perfectly true. Sadler only wished it were the whole truth, and not a mere five per cent of it.

"I was wondering how we're going to get through those mountains," he remarked, pointing to the burning peaks ahead. "Do we go over—or under?"

"Over," said Molton. "They look spectacular, but they're really not so big. Wait till you see the Leibnitz Mountains or the Oberth Range. They're twice as high."

These are quite good enough to start with, thought Sadler. The low-slung monorail car, straddling its single track, bored through the shadows on a slowly rising course. In the darkness around them, dimly seen crags and cliffs rushed forward with explosive swiftness, then vanished astern. Sadler realized that probably nowhere else could one travel at such velocities so close to the ground. No jet liner, far above the clouds of Earth, ever gave such an impression of sheer speed as this.

If it had been day, Sadler could have seen the prodigies of engineering that had flung this track across the foothills of the Apennines. But the darkness veiled the gossamer bridges and the canyon-fringing curves; he saw only the approaching peaks,

4

still magically afloat upon the sea of night that lapped around them.

Then, far to the east, a burning bow peeped above the edge of the Moon. They had risen out of shadow, had joined the mountains in their glory and overtaken the sun itself. Sadler looked away from the glare which flooded the cabin, and for the first time saw clearly the man standing by his side.

Doctor (or would it be Professor?) Molton was in the early fifties, but his hair was quite black and very abundant. He had one of those strikingly ugly faces that somehow immediately inspire confidence. Here, one felt, was the humorous, worldly-wise philosopher, the modern Socrates, sufficiently detached to give unbiased advice to all, yet by no means aloof from human contact. The heart of gold beneath the rugged exterior, Sadler thought to himself, and flinched mentally at the triteness of the phrase.

Their eyes met in the silent appraisal of two men who know that their future business will bring them together again. Then Molton smiled, wrinkling a face that was almost as craggy as the surrounding moonscape.

"Must be your first dawn on the Moon. If you can call this a dawn, of course—anyway, it's a sunrise. Pity it'll only last ten minutes—we'll be over the top then and back into night. Then you'll have to wait two weeks to see the sun again."

"Doesn't it get a trifle—boring—being cooped up for fourteen days?" asked Sadler. No sooner had he spoken the words than he realized that he had probably made a fool of himself. But Molton let him down lightly.

"You'll see," he answered. "Day or night, it's much the same underground. Anyway, you can go out whenever you like. Some people prefer the nighttime; the Earthlight makes them feel romantic."

The monorail had now reached the apex of its trajectory through the mountains. Both travelers fell silent as the peaks on either side reared to their climax, then began to sink astern. They had burst through the barrier, and were dropping down the much steeper slopes overlooking the *Mare Imbrium*. As they descended, so the sun which their speed had conjured back from night shrank from a bow to a thread, from a thread to a

5

single point of fire, and winked out of existence. In the last instant of that false sunset, seconds before they sank again into the shadow of the Moon, there was a moment of magic that Sadler would never forget. They were moving along a ridge that the sun had already left, but the track of the monorail, scarcely a meter above it, still caught the last rays. It seemed as if they were rushing along an unsupported ribbon of light, a filament of flame built by sorcery rather than human engineering. Then final darkness fell, and the magic ended. The stars began to creep back into the sky as Sadler's eyes readapted themselves to the night.

"You were lucky," said Molton. "I've ridden this run a hundred times, but I've never seen that. Better come back into the car—they'll be serving a snack in a minute. Nothing more to see now, anyway."

That, thought Sadler, was hardly true. The blazing Earth-light, coming back into its own now that the sun was gone, flooded the great plain that the ancient astronomers had so inaccurately christened the Sea of Rains. Compared with the mountains that lay behind, it was not spectacular, yet it was still something to catch the breath.

"I'll wait awhile," Sadler answered. "Remember, this is all new to me and I don't want to miss any of it."

Molton laughed, not unkindly. "Can't say I blame you," he said. "Afraid we sometimes take things for granted."

The monorail was now sliding down an absolutely vertiginous incline that would have been suicide on Earth. The cold, greenlit plain lifted to meet them: a range of low hills, dwarfs beside the mountains they had left behind, broke the skyline ahead. Once again, the uncannily near horizon of this little world began to close in upon them. They were back at "sea" level. . . .

Sadler followed Molton through the curtains and into the cabin, where the steward was setting out trays for his small company.

"Do you always have as few passengers as this?" asked Sadler. "I shouldn't think it was a very economical proposition."

"Depends what you mean by economical," Molton replied. "A lot of the things here will look funny on your balance

6

sheets. But it doesn't cost much to run this service. Equipment lasts forever—no rust, no weather. Cars get serviced only every couple of years."

That was something Sadler certainly hadn't considered. There were a great many things he had to learn, and some of them he might find out the hard way.

The meal was tasty but unidentifiable. Like all food on the Moon, it would have been grown in the great hydroponic farms that sprawled their square kilometers of pressurized greenhouses along the equator. The meat course was presumably synthetic: it might have been beef, but Sadler happened to know that the only cow on the Moon lived in luxury at the Hipparchus Zoo. This was the sort of useless information his diabolically retentive mind was always picking up and refusing to disgorge.

Perhaps mealtime had made the other astronomers more affable, for they were friendly enough when Dr. Molton introduced them, and managed to avoid talking shop for a few minutes. It was obvious, however, that they regarded his mission with some alarm. Sadler could see them all mentally reviewing their appropriations and wondering what kind of case they could put up if they were challenged. He had no doubt that they would all have highly convincing stories, and would try to blind him with science if he attempted to pin them down. He had been through it all before, though never in quite such circumstances as these.

The car was now on the last lap of its journey, and would be at the Observatory in little more than an hour. The six-hundred-kilometer run across the *Mare Imbrium* was almost straight and level, apart from a brief detour to the east to avoid the hills around the giant walled-plain of Archimedes. Sadler settled himself down comfortably, pulled out his briefing papers, and began to do some study.

The organization chart he unfolded covered most of the table. It was neatly printed in several colors, according to the various departments of the Observatory, and Sadler looked at it with some distaste. Ancient man, he remembered, had once been defined as a tool-making animal. He often felt that the

7

best description of modern man would be a paper-wasting animal.

Below the headings "Director and "Deputy Director" the chart split three ways under the captions ADMINISTRATION, TECHNICAL SERVICES, and OBSERVATORY. Sadler looked for Dr. Molton; yes, there he was, in the OBSERVATORY section, directly beneath the chief scientist and heading the short column of names labeled "Spectroscopy." He seemed to have six assistants: two of them—Jamieson and Wheeler—were men to whom Sadler had just been introduced. The other traveler in the monocab, he discovered, was not really a scientist at all. He had a little box of his own on the chart, and was responsible to no one but the director. Sadler suspected that Secretary Wagnall was probably quite a power in the land, and would be well worth cultivating.

He had been studying the chart for half an hour, and had completely lost himself in its ramifications, when someone switched on the radio. Sadler had no objection to the soft music that filled the car; his powers of concentration could deal with worse interference than this. Then the music stopped; there was a brief pause, the six beeps of a time signal, and a suave voice began:

"This is Earth, Channel Two, Interplanetary Network. The signal you have just heard was twenty-one hundred hours G.M.T. Here is the news."

There was no trace of interference. The words were as clear as if they were coming from a local station. Yet Sadler had noticed the skyward tilting antenna system on the roof of the monocab, and knew that he was listening to a direct transmission. The words he was hearing had left Earth almost one and a half seconds ago. Already they would be heading past him to far more distant worlds. There would be men who would not hear them for minutes yet—perhaps for hours, if the ships that the Federation had beyond Saturn were listening in. And that voice from Earth would still go on, expanding and fading, far beyond the uttermost limits of man's explorations, until somewhere on the way to Alpha Centauri it was at last obliterated by the ceaseless radio whispering of the stars themselves.

"Here is the news. It has just been announced from the Hague that the conference on planetary resources has broken down. The delegates of the Federation are leaving Earth tomorrow, and the following statement has been issued from the office of the President. . . ."

There was nothing here that Sadler had not expected. But when a fear, however long anticipated, turns into a fact, there is always that same sinking of the heart. He glanced at his companions. Did they realize how serious this was?

They did. Secretary Wagnall had his chin cupped fiercely in his hands; Dr. Molton was leaning back in his chair, eyes closed; Jamieson and Wheeler were staring at the table in glum concentration. Yes, they understood. Their work and their remoteness from Earth had not isolated them from the main currents of human affairs.

The impersonal voice, with its catalogue of disagreements and countercharges, of threats barely veiled by the euphemisms of diplomacy, seemed to bring the inhuman cold of the lunar night seeping through the walls. It was hard to face the bitter truth, and millions of men would still be living in a fool's paradise. They would shrug their shoulders and say with forced cheerfulness, "Don't worry—it will all blow over."

Sadler did not believe so. As he sat in that little, brightly illuminated cylinder racing north across the Sea of Rains, he knew that for the first time in two hundred years humanity was faced with the threat of war.

Chapter II

IF WAR CAME, thought Sadler, it would be a tragedy of circumstances rather than deliberate policy. Indeed, the stubborn fact that had brought Earth into conflict with her ex-colonies sometimes seemed to him like a bad joke on the part of Nature.

Even before his unwelcome and unexpected assignment, Sadler had been well aware of the main facts behind the current crisis. It had been developing for more than a generation, and it arose from the peculiar position of the planet Earth.

9

The human race had been born on a world unique in the solar system, loaded with a mineral wealth unmatched elsewhere. This accident of fate had given a flying start to man's technology, but when he reached the other planets, he found to his surprise and disappointment that for many of his most vital needs he must still depend on the home world.

Earth is the densest of all the planets, only Venus approaching it in this respect. But Venus has no satellite, and the Earth-Moon system forms a double world of a type found nowhere else among the planets. Its mode of formation is a mystery still, but it is known that when Earth was molten the Moon circled at only a fraction of its present distance, and raised gigantic tides in the plastic substance of its companion.

As a result of these internal tides, the crust of the Earth is rich in heavy metals—far richer than that of any other of the planets: They hoard their wealth far down within their unreachable cores, protected by pressures and temperatures that guard them from man's depredations. So as human civilization spread outward from Earth, the drain on the mother world's dwindling resources steadily increased.

The light elements existed on the other planets in unlimited amounts, but such essential metals as mercury, lead, uranium, platinum, thorium and tungsten were almost unobtainable. For many of them no substitutes existed; their large-scale synthesis was impractical, despite two centuries of effort—and modern technology could not survive without them.

It was an unfortunate situation, and a very galling one for the independent republics on Mars, Venus and the larger satellites, which had now united to form the Federation. It kept them dependent upon Earth, and prevented their expansion toward the frontiers of the solar system. Though they had searched among the asteroids and moons, among the rubble left over when the worlds were formed, they had found little but worthless rock and ice. They must go cap in hand to the mother planet for almost every gram of a dozen metals that were more precious than gold.

That in itself might not have been serious, had not Earth grown steadily more jealous of its offspring during the two hundred years since the dawn of space travel. It was, thought

Sadler, an old, old story, perhaps its classic example being the case of England and the American colonies. It has been truly said that history never repeats itself, but historical situations recur. The men who governed Earth were far more intelligent than George the Third; nevertheless, they were beginning to show the same reactions as that unfortunate monarch.

There were excuses on both sides; there always are. Earth was tired; it had spent itself, sending out its best blood to the stars. It saw power slipping from its hands, and knew that it had already lost the future. Why should it speed the process by giving to its rivals the tools they needed?

The Federation, on the other hand, looked back with a kind of affectionate contempt upon the world from which it had sprung. It had lured to Mars, Venus and the satellites of the giant planets some of the finest intellects and the most adventurous spirits of the human race. Here was the new frontier, one that would expand forever toward the stars. It was the greatest physical challenge mankind had ever faced, it could be met only by supreme scientific skill and unyielding determination. These were virtues no longer essential on Earth; the fact that Earth was well aware of it did nothing to ease the situation.

All this might lead to discord and interplanetary invective, but it could never lead to violence. Some other factor was needed to produce that, some final spark which would set off an explosion echoing round the solar system.

That spark had now been struck. The world did not know it yet, and Sadler himself had been equally ignorant a short six months ago. Central Intelligence, the shadowy organization of which he was now a reluctant member, had been working night and day to neutralize the damage. A mathematical thesis entitled "A Quantitative Theory of the Formation of the Lunar Surface Features" did not look like the sort of thing that could start a war—but an equally theoretical paper by a certain Albert Einstein had once ended one.

The paper had been written about two years ago by Professor Roland Phillips, a peaceable Oxford cosmologist with no interest in politics. He had submitted it to the Royal Astronomical Society, and it was now becoming a little difficult to give him a satisfactory explanation of the delay in publication.

11

Unfortunately—and this was the fact that caused great distress to Central Intelligence—Professor Phillips had innocently sent copies to his colleagues on Mars and Venus. Desperate attempts had been made to intercept them, but in vain. By now, the Federation must know that the Moon was not as impoverished a world as had been believed for two hundred years.

There was no way of calling back knowledge that had leaked out, but there were other things about the Moon which it was now equally important that the Federation should not learn. Yet somehow it was learning them; somehow, information was leaking across space from Earth to Moon, and then out to the planets.

When there's a leak in the house, thought Sadler, you send for the plumber. But how do you deal with a leak which you can't see—and which may be anywhere on the surface of a world as large as Africa?

He still knew very little about the scope, size and methods of Central Intelligence—and still resented, futile though that was, the way in which his private life had been disrupted. By training, he was precisely what he pretended to be—an accountant. Six months ago, for reasons which had not been explained and which he probably never would discover, he had been interviewed and offered an unspecified job. His acceptance was quite voluntary; it was merely made clear to him that he had better not refuse. Since then he had spent most of his time under hypnosis, being pumped full of the most various kinds of information and living a monastic life in an obscure corner of Canada. (At least, he thought it was Canada, but it might equally well have been Greenland or Siberia.) Now he was here on the Moon, a minor pawn in a game of interplanetary chess. He would be very glad when the whole frustrating experience was over. It seemed quite incredible to him that anyone would ever *voluntarily* become a secret agent. Only very immature and unbalanced individuals could get any satisfaction from such frankly uncivilized behavior.

There were a few compensations. In the ordinary way, he would never have had a chance of going to the Moon, and the experience he was gathering now might be a real asset in later years. Sadler always tried to take the long view, particularly when he was depressed by the current situation. And the situation, both on the personal and interplanetary levels, was depressing enough.

The safety of Earth was quite a responsibility, but it was really too big for one man to worry about. Whatever reason said, the vast imponderables of planetary politics were less of a burden than the little cares of everyday life. To a cosmic observer, it might have seemed very quaint that Sadler's greatest worry concerned one solitary human being. Would Jeannette ever forgive him, he wondered, for being away on their wedding anniversary? At least she would expect him to call her, and that was the one thing he dared not do. As far as his wife and his friends were concerned, he was still on Earth. There was no way of calling from the Moon without revealing his location, for the two-and-a-half-second time-lag would betray him at once.

Central Intelligence could fix many things, but it could hardly speed up radio waves. It could deliver his anniversary present on time, as it had promised—but it couldn't tell Jeannette when he would be home again.

And it couldn't change the fact that, to conceal his whereabouts, he had had to lie to his wife in the sacred name of Security.

Chapter III

WHEN CONRAD WHEELER had finished comparing the tapes, he got up from his chair and walked three times round the room. From the way he moved, an old hand could have told that Wheeler was a relative newcomer to the Moon. He had been with the Observatory staff for just six months, and still overcompensated for the fractional gravity in which he now lived. There was a jerkiness about his movements that contrasted with the smooth, almost slow-motion gait of his colleagues. Some of this abruptness was due to his own temperament, his lack of discipline, and quickness at jumping to conclusions. It was that temperament he was now trying to guard against.

He had made mistakes before—but this time, surely, there could be no doubt. The facts were undisputed, the calculation trivial—the answer awe-inspiring. Far out in the depths of space, a star had exploded with unimaginable violence. Wheeler looked at the figures he had jotted down, checked them for the tenth time, and reached for the phone.

Sid Jamieson was not pleased at the interruption. "Is it really important?" he queried. "I'm in the darkroom, doing some stuff for Old Mole. I'll have to wait until these plates are washing, anyway."

"How long will that take?"

"Oh, maybe five minutes. Then I've got some more to do."

"I think this *is* important. It'll only take a moment. I'm up in Instrumentation 5."

Jamieson was still wiping developer from his hands when he arrived. After more than three hundred years, certain aspects of photography were quite unchanged. Wheeler, who thought that everything could be done by electronics, regarded many of his older friend's activities as survivals from the age of alchemy.

"Well?" said Jamieson, as usual wasting no words.

Wheeler pointed to the punched tape lying on the desk.

"I was doing the routine check of the magnitude integrator. It's found something."

"It's always doing *that*," snorted Jamieson. "Every time anyone sneezes in the Observatory, it thinks it's discovered a new planet."

There were solid grounds for Jamieson's skepticism. The integrator was a tricky instrument, easily misled, and many astronomers thought it more trouble than it was worth. But it happened to be one of the director's pet projects, so there was no hope of doing anything about it until there was a change of administration. Maclaurin had invented it himself, back in the days when he had had time to do some practical astronomy. An automatic watchdog of the skies, it would wait patiently for years until a new star—a "nova"—blazed in the heavens. Then it would ring a bell and start calling for attention.

14

"Look," said Wheeler, "there's the record. Don't just take my word for it."

Jamieson ran the tape through the converter, copied down the figures and did a quick calculation. Wheeler smiled in satisfaction and relief as his friend's jaw dropped.

"Thirteen magnitudes in twenty-four hours! Wow!"

"I made it thirteen point four, but that's good enough. For my money, it's a supernova. And a close one."

The two young astronomers looked at each other in thoughtful silence. Then Jamieson remarked:

"This is too good to be true. Don't start telling everybody about it until we're quite sure. Let's get its spectrum first, and treat it as an ordinary nova until then."

There was a dreamy look in Wheeler's eyes.

"When was the last supernova in our galaxy?"

"That was Tycho's star—no it wasn't—there was one a bit later, round about 1600."

"Anyway, it's been a long time. This ought to get me on good terms with the director again."

"Perhaps," said Jamieson dryly. "It would just about take a supernova to do that. I'll go and get the spectrograph ready while you put out the report. We mustn't be greedy; the other observatories will want to get into the act." He looked at the integrator, which had returned to its patient searching of the sky. "I guess you've paid for yourself," he added, "even if you never find anything again except spaceship navigation lights."

Sadler heard the news without particular excitement in the Common Room an hour later. He was too preoccupied with his own problems and the mountain of work which faced him to take much notice of the Observatory's routine program, even when he fully understood it. Secretary Wagnall, however, quickly made it clear that this was very far from being a routine matter.

"Here's something to put on your balance sheet," he said cheerfully. "It's the biggest astronomical discovery for years. Come up to the roof."

Sadler dropped the trenchant editorial in *Time Interplanetary* which he had been reading with growing annoyance. The magazine fell with that dreamlike slowness he had not yet

15

grown accustomed to, and he followed Wagnall to the elevator.

They rose past the residential level, past Administration, past Power and Transport, and emerged into one of the small observation domes. The plastic bubble was scarcely ten meters across, and the awnings that shielded it during the lunar day had been rolled back. Wagnall switched off the internal lights, and they stood looking up at the stars and the waxing Earth. Sadler had been here several times before; he knew no better cure for mental fatigue.

A quarter of a kilometer away the great framework of the largest telescope ever built by man was pointing steadily toward a spot in the southern sky. Sadler knew that it was looking at no stars that his eyes could see—at no stars, indeed, that belonged to this universe. It would be probing the limits of space, a billion light-years from home.

Then, unexpectedly, it began to swing toward the north. Wagnall chuckled quietly.

"A lot of people will be tearing their hair now," he said. "We've interrupted the program to turn the big guns on *Nova Draconis*. Let's see if we can find it."

He searched for a little while, consulting a sketch in his hand. Sadler, also staring into the north, could see nothing in the least unusual. All the stars there looked just the same to him. But presently, following Wagnall's instructions, and using the Great Bear and Polaris as guides, he found the faint star low down in the northern sky. It was not at all impressive, even if you realized that a couple of days before only the largest telescopes could have found it, and that it had climbed in brilliance a hundred thousand times in a few hours.

Perhaps Wagnall sensed his disappointment.

"It may not look very spectacular now," he said defensively, "but it's still on the rise. With any luck, we may really see something in a day or two."

Day lunar or day terrestrial? Sadler wondered. It was rather confusing, like so many things here. All the clocks ran on a twenty-four hour system and kept Greenwich Mean Time. One minor advantage of this was that one had only to glance at the Earth to get a reasonably accurate time check. But it meant that the progress of light and dark on the lunar surface had no connection at all with what the clocks might say. The sun could be anywhere above or below the horizon when the clocks said it was noon.

Sadler glanced away from the north, back to the Observatory. He had always assumed—without bothering to think about it—that any observatory would consist of a cluster of giant domes, and had forgotten that here on the weatherless Moon there would be no purpose in enclosing the instruments. The thousand centimeter reflector and its smaller companion stood naked and unprotected in the vacuum of space. Only their fragile masters remained underground in the warmth and air of this buried city.

The horizon was almost flat in all directions. Though the Observatory was at the center of the great walled-plain of Plato, the mountain ring was hidden by the curve of the Moon. It was a bleak and desolate prospect, without even a few hills to give it interest. Only a dusty plain, studded here and there with blow-holes and craterlets—and the enigmatic works of man, straining at the stars and trying to wrest away their secrets.

As they left, Sadler glanced once more toward *Draco*, but already he had forgotten which of the faint circumpolar stars was the one he had come to see. "Exactly why," he said to Wagnall, as tactfully as he could—for he did not want to hurt the secretary's feelings—"is this star so important?"

Wagnall looked incredulous, then pained, then understanding.

"Well," he began, "I guess stars are like people. The well-behaved ones never attract much attention. They teach us something, of course, but we can learn a lot more from the ones that go off the rails."

"And do stars do that sort of thing fairly often?"

"Every year about a hundred blow up in our galaxy alone, but those are only ordinary novae. At their peak, they may be above a hundred thousand times as bright as the sun. A *supernova* is a very much rarer, and a very much more exciting affair. We still don't know what causes it, but when a star goes super it may become several *billion* times brighter than the sun. In fact, it can outshine all the other stars in the galaxy added together."

17

Sadler considered this for a while. It was certainly a thought calculated to inspire a moment's silent reflection.

"The important thing is," Wagnall continued eagerly, "that nothing like this has happened since telescopes were invented. The last supernova in *our* universe was six hundred years ago. There have been plenty in other galaxies, but they're too far away to be studied properly. This one, as it were, is right on our doorstep. That fact will be pretty obvious in a couple of days. In a few hours it will be outshining everything in the sky, except the sun and Earth."

"And what do you expect to learn from it?"

"A supernova explosion is the most titanic event known to occur in nature. We'll be able to study the behavior of matter under conditions that make the middle of an atom bomb look like a dead calm. But if you're one of those people who always want a practical use for everything, surely it's of considerable interest to find what makes a star explode? One day, after all, our sun may decide to do likewise."

"And in *that* case," retorted Sadler, "I'd really prefer not to know about it in advance. I wonder if that nova took any planets with it?"

"There's absolutely no way of telling. But it must happen fairly often, because at least one star in ten's got planets."

It was a heart-freezing thought. At any moment, as likely as not, *somewhere* in the universe a whole solar system, with strangely peopled worlds and civilizations, was being tossed carelessly into a cosmic furnace. Life was a fragile and delicate phenomenon, poised on the razor's edge between cold and heat.

But Man was not content with the hazards that Nature could provide. He was busily building his own funeral pyre.

The same thought had occurred to Dr. Molton, but unlike Sadler he could set against it a more cheerful one. *Nova Draconis* was more than two thousand light-years away; the flash of the detonation had been traveling since the birth of Christ. In that time, it must have swept through millions of solar systems, have alerted the inhabitants of a thousand worlds. Even at this moment, scattered over the surface of a sphere four thousand light-years in diameter, there must surely be other astrono-

18

mers, with instruments not unlike his own, who would be trapping the radiations of this dying sun as they ebbed out toward the frontiers of the universe. And it was stranger still to think that infinitely more distant observers, so far away that to them the whole galaxy was no more than a faint smudge of light, would notice some hundred million years from now that our island universe had momentarily doubled its brilliance. . . .

Dr. Molton stood at the control desk in the softly lit chamber that was his laboratory and workshop. It had once been little different from any of the other cells that made up the Observatory, but its occupant had stamped his personality upon it. In one corner stood a vase of artificial flowers, something both incongruous and welcome in such a place as this. It was Molton's only eccentricity, and no one grudged it to him. Since the native lunar vegetation gave such little scope for ornament, he was forced to use creations of wax and wire, skillfully made up for him in Central City. Their arrangement he varied with such ingenuity and resource that he never seemed to have the same flowers on two successive days.

Sometimes Wheeler used to make fun of him about this hobby, claiming that it proved he was homesick and wanted to get back to Earth. It had, in fact, been more than three years since Dr. Molton had returned to his native Australia, but he seemed in no hurry to do so. As he pointed out, there were about a hundred lifetimes of work for him here, and he preferred to let his leave accumulate until he felt like taking it in one installment.

The flowers were flanked by metal filing cases containing the thousands of spectrograms which Molton had gathered during his research. He was not, as he was always careful to point out, a theoretical astronomer. He simply looked and recorded; other people had the task of explaining what he found. Sometimes indignant mathematicians would arrive protesting that no star could *possibly* have a spectrum like this. Then Molton would go to his files, check that there had been no mistake, and reply, "Don't blame me. Take it up with old Mother Nature."

The rest of the room was a crowded mass of equipment that would have been completely meaningless to a layman, and indeed would have baffled many astronomers. Most of it Molton had built himself, or at least designed and handed over to his assistants for construction. For the last two centuries, every practical astronomer had had to be something of an electrician, an engineer, a physicist—and, as the cost of his equipment steadily increased, a public-relations man.

The electronic commands sped silently through the cables as Molton set Right Ascension and Declination. Far above his head, the great telescope, like some mammoth gun, tracked smoothly round to the north. The vast mirror at the base of the tube was gathering more than a million times as much light as a human eye could grasp, and focusing it with exquisite precision into a single beam. That beam, reflected again from mirror to mirror as if down a periscope, was now reaching Dr. Molton, to do with as he pleased.

Had he looked into the beam, the sheer glare of *Nova Draconis* would have blinded him—and as compared with his instruments, his eyes could tell him practically nothing. He switched the electronic spectrometer into place, and started it scanning. It would explore the spectrum of *N. Draconis* with patient accuracy, working down through yellow, green, blue into the violet and far ultra-violet, utterly beyond range of the human eye. As it scanned, it would trace on moving tape the intensity of every spectral line, leaving an unchallengeable record which astronomers could still consult a thousand years from now.

There was a knock at the door and Jamieson entered, carrying some still-damp photographic plates.

"Those last exposures did it!" he said jubilantly. "They show the gaseous shell expanding round the nova. And the speed agrees with your Doppler shifts."

"So I should hope," growled Molton. "Let's look at them."

He studied the plates, while in the background the whirring of electric motors continued from the spectrometer as it kept up its automatic search. They were negatives, of course, but like all astronomers he was accustomed to that and could interpret them as easily as positive prints.

There at the center was the little disk that marked *N. Draconis,* burnt through the emulsion by overexposure. And around it, barely visible to the naked eye, was a tenuous ring. As the

days passed, Molton knew, that ring would
further into space until it was finally dissip
small and insignificant that the mind could
what it really was.

They were looking into the past, at a catastrop
happened two thousand years ago. They were seeing
of flame, so hot that it had not yet cooled to white-heat
the star had blasted into space at millions of kilomete
hour. That expanding wall of fire would have engulfed
mightiest planet without checking its speed; yet from Earth
was no more than a faint ring at the limits of visibility.

"I wonder," said Jamieson softly, "if we'll ever find out just
why a star does this sort of thing?"

"Sometimes," replied Molton, "as I'm listening to the radio,
I think it would be a good idea if it did happen. Fire's a good
sterilizer."

Jamieson was obviously shocked; this was unlike Molton,
whose brusque exterior so inadequately concealed his deep
inner warmth.

"You don't really mean that!" he protested.

"Well, perhaps not. We've made some progress in the past
million years, and I suppose an astronomer should be patient.
But look at the mess we're running into now—don't you ever
wonder how it's all going to end?"

There was a passion, a depth of feeling behind the words
that astonished Jamieson and left him profoundly disturbed.
Molton had never before let down his guard—had never, indeed, indicated that he felt very strongly on any subject outside
his own field. Jamieson knew he had glimpsed the momentary
weakening of an iron control. It stirred something in his own
mind, and mentally he reacted like a startled animal against the
shock of recognition.

For a long moment the two scientists stared at each other,
appraising, speculating, reaching out across the gulf that sepa-
rates every man from his neighbor. Then, with a shrill buzzing,
the automatic spectrometer announced that it had finished its
task. The tension had broken; the everyday world crowded in
upon them again. And so a moment that might have widened

IV

to expect an office of his
as a modest desk in some
that was exactly what he had
by him; he was anxious to cause no trouble
draw no unnecessary attention to himself, and in any
case he spent relatively little time at his desk. All the final
writing up of his reports took place in the privacy of his room
—a tiny cubicle just large enough to ward off claustrophobia,
which was one of a hundred identical cells on the residential
level.

It had taken him several days to adapt to this completely
artificial way of life. Here in the heart of the Moon, time
did not exist. The fierce temperature changes between the
lunar day and night penetrated no more than a meter or two
into the rock; the diurnal waves of heat and cold ebbed away
before they reached this depth. Only Man's clocks ticked off
the seconds and minutes; every twenty-four hours the corridor
lights dimmed, and there was a pretense of night. Even then
the Observatory did not sleep. Whatever the hour, there would
be someone on duty. The astronomers, of course, had always
been accustomed to working at peculiar hours, much to the
annoyance of their wives (except in those quite common
cases where the wives were astronomers too). The rhythm of
lunar life was no additional hardship to them; the ones who
grumbled were the engineers who had to maintain air, power,
communications and the Observatory's other multitudinous
services on a twenty-four-hour basis.

On the whole, thought Sadler, the administrative staff had
the best of it. It did not matter much if Accounts, Entertainment or Stores closed down for eight hours, as they did in every
twenty-four, so long as someone continued to run the surgery
and the kitchen.

Sadler had done his best not to get in anyone's hair, and believed that so far he had been quite successful. He had met all the senior staff except the director himself—who was absent on Earth—and knew by sight about half the people in the Observatory. His plan had been to work conscientiously from section to section until he had seen everything the place had to offer. When he had done that, he would sit and think for a couple of days. There were some jobs which simply could not be hurried, whatever the urgency.

Urgency—yes, that was his main problem. Several times he had been told, not unkindly, that he had come to the Observatory at a very awkward time. The mounting political tension had set the little community's nerves on edge, and tempers had been growing short. It was true that *Nova Draconis* had improved the situation somewhat, since no one could be bothered with such trivialities as politics while this phenomenon blazed in the skies. But they could not be bothered with cost accounting either, and Sadler could hardly blame them.

He spent all the time he could spare from his investigation in the Common Room, where the staff relaxed when they were off duty. Here was the center of the Observatory's social life, and it gave him an ideal opportunity of studying the men and women who had exiled themselves here for the good of science —or, alternatively, for the inflated salaries required to lure less dedicated individuals to the Moon.

Though Sadler was not addicted to gossip, and was more interested in facts and figures than in people, he knew that he had to make the most of this opportunity. Indeed, his instructions had been very specific on this point, in a manner he considered unnecessarily cynical. But it could not be denied that human nature is always very much the same, among all classes and on all planets. Sadler had picked up some of his most useful information simply by standing within earshot of the bar. . . .

The Common Room had been designed with great skill and taste, and the constantly changing photo-murals made it hard to believe that this spacious chamber was, in reality, deep in the crust of the Moon. As a whim of the architect, there was an open fire in which a most realistic pile of logs burned for-

23

ever without being consumed. This quite fascinated Sadler, who had never seen anything like it on Earth.

He had now shown himself sufficiently good at games and general conversation to become an accepted member of the staff, and had even been entrusted with much of the local scandal. Apart from the fact that its members were of distinctly superior intelligence, the Observatory was a microcosm of Earth itself. With the exception of murder (and *that* was probably only a matter of time) almost everything that happened in terrestrial society was going on somewhere here. Sadler was seldom surprised by anything, and certainly not by this. It was merely to be expected that all six of the girls in Computing, after some weeks in a largely male community, now had reputations that could only be described as fragile. Nor was it remarkable that the chief engineer was not on speaking terms with the assistant chief executive, or that Professor X thought that Dr. Y was a certifiable lunatic, or that Mr. Z was reputed to cheat at Hypercanasta. All these items were no direct concern of Sadler's, though he listened to them with great interest. They merely went to prove that the Observatory was one big happy family.

Sadler was wondering what humorist had stamped NOT TO BE TAKEN OUT OF THE LOUNGE across the shapely lady on the cover of last month's *Triplanet News* when Wheeler came storming into the room.

"What is it now?" asked Sadler. "Discovered another nova? Or just looking for a shoulder to weep on?"

He rather guessed that the latter was the case, and that his shoulder would have to do in the absence of anything more suitable. By this time he had grown to know Wheeler quite well. The young astronomer might be one of the most junior members of the staff, but he was also the most memorable. His sarcastic wit, lack of respect for higher authority, confidence in his own opinions and general argumentativeness prevented him from hiding his light under a bushel. But Sadler had been told, even by those who did not like Wheeler, that he was brilliant and would go far. At the moment he had not used up the stock of good will created by his discovery of *Nova Dra-*

conis, which in itself would be enough to insure a reputation for the rest of his career.

"I was looking for Wagtail; he's not in his office, and I want to lodge a complaint."

"Secretary Wagnall," answered Sadler, putting as much reproof as he could into the correction, "went over to Hydroponics half an hour ago. And if I may make a comment, isn't it somewhat unusual for you to be the source, rather than the cause, of a complaint?"

Wheeler gave a large grin, which made him look incredibly and disarmingly boyish.

"I'm afraid you're right. And I know this ought to go through the proper channels, and all that sort of thing—but it's rather urgent. I've just had a couple of hours' work spoiled by some fool making an unauthorized landing."

Sadler had to think quickly before he realized what Wheeler meant. Then he remembered that this part of the Moon was a restricted area: no ships were supposed to fly over the northern hemisphere without first notifying the Observatory. The blinding glare of ion rockets picked up by one of the great telescopes could ruin photographic exposures and play havoc with delicate instruments.

"You don't suppose it was an emergency?" Sadler asked, struck by a sudden thought. "It's too bad about your work, but that ship may be in trouble."

Wheeler had obviously not thought of this, and his rage instantly abated. He looked helplessly at Sadler, as if wondering what to do next. Sadler dropped his magazine and rose to his feet.

"Shouldn't we go to Communications?" he said. "They ought to know what's going on. Mind if I come along?"

He was very particular about such points in etiquette, and never forgot that he was here very much on sufferance. Besides, it was always good policy to let people think they were doing you favors.

Wheeler jumped at the suggestion, and led the way to Communications as if the whole idea had been his own. The signals office was a large, spotlessly tidy room at the highest level of the Observatory, only a few meters below the lunar

25

crust. Here was the automatic telephone exchange, which was the Observatory's central nervous system, and here were the monitors and transmitters which kept this remote scientific outpost in touch with Earth. They were all presided over by the duty signals officer, who discouraged casual visitors with a large notice reading: POSITIVELY AND ABSOLUTELY NO ADMITTANCE TO UNAUTHORIZED PERSONS.

"That doesn't mean us," said Wheeler, opening the door. He was promptly contradicted by a still larger notice—THIS MEANS YOU. Unabashed, he turned to the grinning Sadler and added, "All the places you're *really* not supposed to enter are kept locked, anyway." Nevertheless he did not push open the second door, but knocked and waited until a bored voice called "Come in."

The D.S.O., who was dissecting a spacesuit walkie-talkie set, seemed quite glad for the interruption. He promptly called Earth and asked Traffic Control to find out what a ship was doing in the *Mare Imbrium* without notifying the Observatory. While they were waiting for the reply to come back, Sadler wandered round the racks of equipment.

It was really surprising that it needed so much apparatus just to talk to people, or to send pictures between Moon and Earth. Sadler, who knew how technicians loved explaining their work to anyone who showed real interest, asked a few questions and tried to absorb as many of the answers as he could. He was thankful that by this time no one bothered to wonder if he had any ulterior motives and was trying to find if they could do their jobs for half the money. They had accepted him as an interested and inquisitive audience of one, for it was quite obvious that many of the questions he asked could have no financial significance.

The reply from Earth came through on the auto-printer soon after the D.S.O. had finished his swift conducted tour. It was a slightly baffling message:

FLIGHT NON-SCHEDULED. GOVERNMENT BUSINESS. NO NOTIFICATION ISSUED. FURTHER LANDINGS ANTICIPATED. INCONVENIENCE REGRETTED.

Wheeler looked at the words as if he could not believe his eyes. Until this moment, the skies of the Observatory had been sacrosanct. No abbot facing the violation of his monastery could have been more indignant.

"They're going to keep it up!" he spluttered. "What about our program?"

"Grow up, Con," said the signals officer indulgently. "Don't you listen to the news? Or have you been too busy looking at your pet nova? This message means just one thing. There's something secret going on out in the *Mare*. I'll give you one guess."

"I know," said Wheeler. "There's another of those hush-hush expeditions looking for heavy ores, in the hope that the Federation won't find out. It's all so damn childish."

"What makes you think *that's* the explanation?" asked Sadler sharply.

"Well, that sort of thing's been going on for years. Any bar in town will give you all the latest gossip."

Sadler hadn't been "into town" yet—as the trip to Central City was called—but he could well believe this. Wheeler's explanation was highly plausible, particularly in view of the current situation.

"We'll just have to make the best of it, I suppose," said the D.S.O., attacking his walkie-talkie again. "Anyway, there's one consolation. All this is going on to the south of us—the other side of the sky from Draco. So it won't really interfere with your main work, will it?"

"I suppose not," Wheeler admitted grudgingly. For a moment he seemed quite downcast. It was not—far from it—that he wanted anything to interfere with work. But he had been looking forward to a good fight, and to have it snatched out of his hands like this was a bitter disappointment.

It needed no knowledge of the stars to see *Nova Draconis* now. Next to the waxing Earth, it was by far the brightest object in the sky. Even Venus, following the sun into the east, was pale compared to this arrogant newcomer. Already it had begun to cast a distinct shadow and it was still growing in brilliance.

Down on Earth, according to the reports coming over the radio, it was clearly visible even in the daytime. For a little while it had crowded politics off the front page, but now the pressure of events was making itself felt again. Men could not bear to think of eternity for long; and the Federation was only light-minutes, not light-centuries, away.

Chapter V

THERE WERE STILL those who believed that Man would have been happier had he stayed on his own planet; but it was rather too late, now, to do anything about that. In any case, had he remained on Earth, he would not have been Man. The restlessness that had driven him over the face of his own world, that had made him climb the skies and plumb the seas, would not be assuaged while the Moon and planets beckoned to him across the deeps of space.

The colonization of the Moon had been a slow, painful, sometimes tragic and always fabulously expensive enterprise. Two centuries after the first landings, much of Earth's giant satellite was still unexplored. Every detail had, of course, been mapped from space, but more than half that craggy globe had never been examined at close quarters.

Central City and the other bases that had been established with such labor were islands of life in an immense wilderness, oases in a silent desert of blazing light or inky darkness. There had been many who had asked whether the effort needed to survive here was worthwhile, since the colonization of Mars and Venus offered much greater opportunities. But for all the problems it presented him, Man could not do without the Moon. It had been his first bridgehead in space, and was still the key to the planets. The liners that plied from world to world obtained all their propellent mass here, filling their great tanks with the finely divided dust which the ionic rockets would spit out in electrified jets. By obtaining that dust from the Moon, and not having to lift it through the enormous gravity field of Earth, it had been possible to reduce the cost of space-travel more than ten-fold. Indeed, without the Moon as a refueling base, economical space-flight could never have been achieved.

It had also proved, as the astronomers and physicists had predicted, of immense scientific value. Freed at last from the imprisoning atmosphere of Earth, astronomy had made giant strides, and indeed there was scarcely a branch of science that had not benefited from the lunar laboratories. Whatever the limitations of Earth's statesmen, they had learned one lesson well. Scientific research was the lifeblood of civilization; it was the one investment that could be guaranteed to pay dividends for eternity. . . .

Slowly, with countless heartbreaking setbacks, man had discovered how to exist, then to live, and at last to flourish on the Moon. He had invented whole new techniques of vacuum engineering, of low-gravity architecture, of air and temperature control. He had defeated the twin demons of the lunar day and the lunar night, though always he must be on the watch against their depredations. The burning heat could expand his domes and crack his buildings; the fierce cold could tear apart any metal structure not designed to guard against contractions never encountered on Earth. But all these problems had, at last, been overcome.

All novel and ambitious enterprises seem much more hazardous and difficult from afar. So it had proved with the Moon. Problems that had appeared insuperable before the Moon was reached had now passed into lunar folklore. Obstacles that had disheartened the first explorers had been almost forgotten. Over the lands where men had once struggled on foot, the monocabs now carried the tourists from Earth in luxurious comfort. . . .

In a few respects, conditions on the Moon had helped rather than hindered the invaders. There was, for example, the question of the lunar atmosphere. On Earth it would have counted as a good vacuum, and it had no appreciable effect on astronomical observations. It was quite sufficient, however, to act as a very efficient shield against meteors. Most meteors are blocked by Earth's atmosphere before they get to within a hundred kilometers of the surface; they have been checked, in other words, while traveling through air no denser than the Moon's. Indeed, the Moon's invisible meteor shield is even more effective than Earth's, since thanks to the low lunar gravity it extends much farther into space.

Perhaps the most astonishing discovery of the first explorers was the existence of plant life. It had long been suspected, from the peculiar changes of light and shade in such craters as Aristarchus and Eratosthenes, that there was some form of vegetation on the Moon, but it was difficult to see how it could survive under such extreme conditions. Perhaps, it was surmised, a few primitive lichens or mosses might exist, and it would be interesting to see how they managed to do it.

The guess was quite wrong. A little thought would have shown that any lunar plants would not be primitive, but would be highly specialized—extremely sophisticated, in fact, so that they could cope with their hostile environment. Primitive plants could no more exist on the Moon than could primitive Man.

The commonest lunar plants were plump, often globular growths, not unlike cacti. Their horny skins prevented the loss of precious water, and were dotted here and there with transparent "windows" to let sunlight enter. This astonishing improvisation, surprising though it seemed to many, was not unique. It had been evolved independently by certain desert plants in Africa, faced with the same problem of trapping sunlight without losing water.

The unique feature of the lunar plants, however, was their ingenious mechanism for collecting air. An elaborate system of flaps and valves, not unlike that by which some sea creatures pump water through their bodies, acted as kind of compressor. The plants were patient; they would wait for years along the great crevasses which occasionally gush forth feeble clouds of carbon or sulphur dioxides from the Moon's interior. Then the flaps would go frantically to work, and the strange plants would suck into their pores every molecule that drifted by, before the transient lunar mist dispersed into the hungry near-vacuum which was all the atmosphere remaining to the Moon.

Such was the strange world which was now home to some thousands of human beings. For all its harshness, they loved it and would not return to Earth, where life was easy and therefore offered little scope for enterprise or initiative. Indeed, the lunar colony, bound though it was to Earth by economic ties, had more

30

in common with the planets of the Federation. On Mars, Venus, Mercury and the satellites of Jupiter and Saturn, men were fighting a frontier war against Nature, very like that which had won the Moon. Mars was already completely conquered; it was the only world outside Earth where a man could walk in the open without the use of artificial aids. On Venus, victory was in sight, and a land surface three times as great as Earth's would be the prize. Elsewhere, only outposts existed: burning Mercury and the frozen outer worlds were a challenge for future centuries.

So Earth considered. But the Federation could not wait, and Professor Phillips, in complete innocence, had brought its impatience to the breaking point. It was not the first time that a scientific paper had changed the course of history, and it would not be the last.

Sadler had never seen the pages of mathematics that had caused all the trouble, but he knew the conclusions to which they led. He had been taught many things in the six months that had been abstracted from his life. Some he had learned in a small, bare classroom with six other men whose names he had never been told, but much knowledge had come to him in sleep or in the dreamy trance-state of hypnosis. One day, perhaps, it would be withdrawn from him by the same techniques. The face of the Moon, Sadler had been told, consists of two distinct kinds of terrain—the dark areas of the so-called Seas, and the bright regions which are usually higher in elevation and much more mountainous. It is the bright areas which are pitted with the countless lunar craters, and appear to have been torn and blasted by eons of volcanic fury. The Seas, by contrast, are flat and relatively smooth. They contain occasional craters and many pits and crevasses, but they are incomparably more irregular than the rugged highlands.

They were formed, it seems, much later than the mountains and crater chains of the Moon's fiery youth. Somehow, long after the older formations had congealed, the crust melted again in a few areas to form the dark, smooth plains that are the Seas. They contain the wrecks of many older craters and mountains that have been melted down like wax, and their coasts are

31

fringed with half-destroyed cliffs and ringed plains that barely escaped total obliteration.

The problem which had long engaged scientists, and which Professor Phillips had solved, was this: Why did the internal heat of the Moon break out only in the selected areas of the Seas, leaving the ancient highlands untouched?

A planet's internal heat is produced by radioactivity. It seemed to Professor Phillips, therefore, that under the great Seas must be rich deposits of uranium and its associated elements. The ebb and flow of tides in the Moon's molten interior had somehow produced these local concentrations, and the heat they had generated through millennia of radioactivity had melted the surface features far above them to form the Seas.

For two centuries, men had gone over the face of the Moon with every conceivable measuring instrument. They had set its interior trembling with artificial earthquakes; they had probed it with magnetic and electric fields. Thanks to these observations, Professor Phillips had been able to put his theory on a sound mathematical basis.

Vast lodes of uranium existed far below the Seas. Uranium itself was no longer of the vital importance that it had been in the twentieth and twenty-first centuries, for the old fission piles had long since given way to the hydrogen reactor. But where there was uranium, the heavy metals would be found as well.

Professor Phillips had been quite sure that his theory had no practical applications. All these great deposits, he had carefully pointed out, were at such depths that any form of mining would be totally out of the question. They were at least a hundred kilometers down—and the pressure in the rock at that depth was so great that the toughest metal would flow like a liquid, so that no shaft or bore-hole could stay open even for an instant.

It seemed a great pity. These tantalizing treasures, Professor Phillips had concluded, must remain forever beyond the reach of the men who needed them so badly.

A scientist, thought Sadler, should really have known better than that. One day Professor Phillips was going to have a big surprise.

Chapter VI

SADLER LAY IN HIS BUNK and tried to focus his mind on the past week. It was very hard to believe that he had arrived from Earth only eight of its days ago, but the calendar clock on the wall confirmed the notes he had made in his diary. And if he doubted both these witnesses, he had merely to go up to the surface and enter one of the observation domes. There he could look up at the unmoving Earth, now just past full and beginning to wane. When he had arrived on the Moon, it had been at its first quarter.

It was midnight over the *Mare Imbrium.* Dawn and sunset were both equally remote, but the lunar landscape was ablaze with light. Challenging the Earth itself was *Nova Draconis,* already brighter than any star in history. Even Sadler, who found most astronomical events too remote and impersonal to touch his emotions, would occasionally make the trip "upstairs" to look at this new invader of the modern skies. Was he looking at the funeral pyre of worlds older and wiser than the Earth? It was strange that such an awe-inspiring event should take place at a moment of human crisis. It could only be coincidence, of course. *N. Draconis* was a close star, yet the signal of its death had been traveling for twenty centuries. One had to be not only superstitious but also very geocentric to imagine that this event had been planned as a warning for Earth. For what of all the other planets of other suns in whose skies the nova blazed with equal or even greater brilliance?

Sadler called home his wandering thoughts, and concentrated on his proper business. What had he left undone? He had visited every section of the Observatory, and met everyone of importance, with the single exception of the director. Professor Maclaurin was due back from Earth in a day or so, and his absence had, if anything, simplified Sadler's task. When the Boss returned, so everybody had warned him, life would not be quite so free and easy, and everything would have to be done through the Proper Channels. Sadler was used to that, but did not enjoy it any the better.

There was a discreet purr from the speaker in the wall over the bed. Sadler reached out one foot and kicked a switch with the toe of his sandal. He could do this the first time now, but faint scars on the wall were a still-visible memento of his apprenticeship.

"Yes," he said. "Who's that?"

"Transport Section here. I'm closing the list for tomorrow. There are still a couple of seats left—you want to come along?"

"If there's room," Sadler replied. "I don't want any more-deserving causes to suffer."

"O.K.—you're down," said the voice briskly, and clicked off.

Sadler felt only the mildest twinge of conscience. After a week's solid work, he could do with a few hours in Central City. He was not yet due to meet his first contact, and so far all his reports had gone out through the normal mail service, in a form that would have meant nothing to anyone happening to read them. But it was high time he got to know his way around the city, and indeed it would look odd if he took no holidays at all.

His main reason for the trip, however, was purely personal. There was a letter he wanted to post, and he knew that the Observatory mail was being censored by his colleagues in Central Intelligence. By now they must be indifferent to such matters, but he would still prefer to keep his private life to himself.

Central City was twenty kilometers from the spaceport, and Sadler had seen nothing of the lunar metropolis on his arrival. As the monocab—much fuller this time than it had been on the outward journey—pulled once more into the *Sinus Medii*, Sadler no longer felt a complete stranger. He knew, at least by sight, everyone in the car. Almost half the Observatory staff were here; the other half would take their day off next week. Even *Nova Draconis* was not allowed to interfere with this routine, which was based on common sense and sound psychology.

The cluster of great domes began to hump themselves over the horizon. A beacon light burned on the summit of each, but otherwise they were darkened and gave no sign of life. Some,

Sadler knew, could be made transparent when desired. All were opaque now, conserving their heat against the lunar night.

The monocab entered a long tunnel at the base of one of the domes. Sadler had a glimpse of great doors closing behind them —then another set, and yet another. They're taking no chances, he thought to himself, and heartily approved of such caution. Then there was the unmistakable sound of air surging around them, a final door opened ahead, and the vehicle rolled to a halt beside a platform that might have been in any station back on Earth. It gave Sadler quite a shock to look through the window and see people walking around outside without spacesuits. . . .

"Going anywhere in particular?" asked Wagnall as they waited for the crush at the door to subside.

Sadler shook his head.

"No—I just want to wander round and have a look at the place. I want to see where you people manage to spend all your money."

Wagnall obviously couldn't decide whether he was joking or not, and to Sadler's relief did not offer his services as a guide. This was one of the occasions when he would be quite happy to be left on his own.

He walked out of the station and found himself at the top of a large ramp, sloping down into the compact little city. The main level was twenty meters below him. He had not realized that the whole dome was countersunk this far into the lunar plain, thus reducing the amount of roof structure necessary. By the side of the ramp a wide conveyor belt was carrying freight and luggage into the station at a leisurely rate. The nearest buildings were obviously industrial, and though well kept had the slightly seedy appearance which inevitably overtakes anything in the neighborhood of stations or docks.

It was not until Sadler was halfway down the ramp that he realized there was a blue sky overhead, that the sun was shining just behind him, and that there were high cirrus clouds floating far above.

The illusion was so perfect that he had taken it completely for granted, and had forgotten for a moment that this was midnight on the Moon. He stared for a long time into the dizzy depths of that synthetic sky, and could see no flaw in its perfec-

35

tion. Now he understood why the lunar cities insisted upon their expensive domes, when they could just as well have burrowed underground like the Observatory.

There was no risk of getting lost in Central City. With one exception each of the seven interconnected domes was laid out in the same pattern of radiating avenues and concentric ring-roads. The exception was Dome Five, the main industrial and production center, which was virtually one vast factory and which Sadler decided to leave alone.

He wandered at random for some time, going where his stray impulses took him. He wanted to get the "feel" of the place, for he realized it was completely impossible to know the city properly in the short time at his disposal. There was one thing about Central City that struck him at once—it had a personality, a character of its own. No one can say why this is true of some cities and not of others, and Sadler felt a little surprised that it should be of such an artificial environment as this. Then he remembered that *all* cities, whether on Earth or on the Moon, were equally artificial. . . .

The roads were narrow, the only vehicles small, three-wheeled open cars that cruised along at less than thirty kilometers an hour and appeared to be used exclusively for freight rather than pas-sengers. It was some time before Sadler discovered the auto-matic subway that linked the outer six domes in a great ring, passing under the center of each. It was really a glorified con-veyor belt, and moved in a counterclockwise direction only. If you were unlucky, you might have to go right round the city to get to the adjacent dome, but as the circular tour took only about five minutes, this was no great hardship.

The shopping center, and main repository of lunar chic, was in Dome One. Here also lived the senior executives and tech-nicians—the most senior of all in houses of their own. Most of the residential buildings had roof gardens, where plants im-ported from Earth ascended to improbable heights in this low gravity. Sadler kept his eyes open for any lunar vegetation, but saw no signs of it. He did not know that there was a strict rule against bringing the indigenous plants into the domes. An oxy-gen-rich atmosphere, it had been found, over-stimulated them so that they ran riot and promptly died, producing a stench

36

which had to be experienced to be believed when their sulphur-loaded organisms began to decay.

Most of the visitors from Earth were to be found here. Sadler, a selenite of eight days' standing, found himself eying the obvious newcomers with amused contempt. Many of them had hired weight-belts as soon as they entered the city, under the impression that this was the safest thing to do. Sadler had been warned about this fallacy in time, and so had avoided contributing to what was really a mild racket. It was true that if you loaded yourself down with lead, there was less danger of soaring off the ground with incautious steps, and perhaps terminating the trajectory upon your head. But surprisingly few people realized the distinction between weight and inertia which made these belts of such dubious value. When one tried to start moving, or to stop in a hurry, one quickly found that though a hundred kilos of lead might *weigh* only sixteen kilos here, it had exactly the same momentum as it did on Earth.

From time to time, as he made his way through the scanty crowds and roamed from shop to shop, Sadler ran into friends from the Observatory. Some of them were already festooned with parcels as they made up for a week's compulsory saving. Most of the younger members of the staff, male and female, had acquired companions. Sadler surmised that though the Observatory might be self-sufficient in most matters, there were others which demanded some variety.

The clear, bell-like note, thrice repeated, caught him unaware. He looked around him, but could not locate its source. At first it seemed that no one was taking any notice of the signal, whatever it might mean. Then he observed that the streets were slowly clearing—and that the sky was getting darker.

Clouds had come up over the sun. They were black and ragged, their edges flame-fringed as the sunlight spilled past them. Once again, Sadler marveled at the skill with which these images—for they could be nothing else—were projected on the dome. No actual thunderstorm could have seemed more realistic, and when the first rumble rolled round the sky he did not hesitate to look for shelter. Even if the streets had not already emptied themselves, he would have guessed that the organizers of this storm were going to omit none of the details. . . .

The little sidewalk café was crowded with other refugees when the initial drops came down, and the first fiery tongue of lightning licked across the heavens. Sadler could never see lightning without counting the seconds before the thunder peal. It came when he had got to "Six," making it two kilometers away. That, of course, would put it well outside the dome, in the soundless vacuum of space. Oh well, one had to allow some artistic license, and it wasn't fair to quibble over points like this.

Thicker and heavier came the rain, more and more continuous the flashes. The roads were running with water, and for the first time Sadler became aware of the shallow gutters which, if he had seen them before, he had dismissed without a second thought. It was not safe to take *anything* for granted here; you had to keep stopping and asking yourself "What function does this serve—What's it doing here on the Moon? Is it even what I think it is?" Certainly, now he came to consider the matter, a gutter was as unexpected a thing to see in Central City as a snow plow. But perhaps even that——

Sadler turned to his closest neighbor, who was watching the storm with obvious admiration.

"Excuse me," he said, "but how often does this sort of thing happen?"

"About twice a day—lunar day, that is," came the reply. "It's always announced a few hours in advance, so that it won't interfere with business."

"I don't want to be too inquisitive," continued Sadler, fearing that was just what he was, "but I'm surprised at the trouble you've gone to. Surely all this realism isn't necessary?"

"Perhaps not, but we like it. We've got to have some rain, remember, to keep the place clean and deal with the dust. So we try to do it properly."

If Sadler had any doubts on that score, they were dispelled when the glorious double rainbow arched out of the clouds. The last drops spattered on the sidewalk; the thunder dwindled away to an angry, distant mutter. The show was over, and the glistening streets of Central City began to fill with life once more.

Sadler remained in the café for a meal, and after a little hard bargaining managed to get rid of some terrestrial currency at only a trifle below the market rate. The food, somewhat to his surprise, was excellent. Every bit must have been synthesized or grown in the yeast and chlorella tanks, but it had been blended and processed with great skill. The trouble with Earth, Sadler mused, was that it could take food for granted, and seldom gave the matter the attention it deserved. Here, on the other hand, food was not something that a bountiful Nature, with a little prompting, could be relied upon to provide. It had to be designed and produced from scratch, and since the job *had* to be done, someone had seen that it was done properly. Like the weather, in fact. . . .

It was time he moved. The last mail for Earth would be cleared in two hours, and if he missed it Jeannette would not get his letter for almost a week of Earth time. She had already been in suspense long enough.

He pulled the unsealed letter from his pocket, and read it through again for any final amendments.

"Jeannette, my dearest,

"I wish I could tell you where I am, but I'm not allowed to say. It wasn't my idea, but I've been chosen for a special job and I've got to make the best of it. I'm in good health, and though I can't contact you directly, any letters you send to the Box Number I gave you will reach me sooner or later.

"I hated being away on our anniversary, but believe me there was *absolutely nothing* I could do about it. I hope you received my present safely—and I hope you liked it. It took me a long time to find that necklace, and I won't tell you how much it cost!

"Do you miss me very badly? God, how I wish I was home again! I know you were hurt and upset when I left, but I want you to trust me and to understand that I couldn't tell you what was happening. Surely you realize that I want Jonathan Peter as much as you do. Please have faith in me, and don't think that it was because of selfishness, or because I don't love you, that I acted as I did. I had very good reasons, which one day I'll be able to tell you.

"Above all, don't worry, and don't be impatient. You know that I'll get back as soon as I can. And I promise you this—

when I'm home again, we'll go ahead. I wish I knew how soon that would be!

"I love you, my darling—don't ever doubt that. This is a tough job, and your faith in me is the one thing that keeps me going."

He read the letter with great care, trying for the moment to forget all that it meant to him, and to regard it as a message that a complete stranger might have written. Did it give too much away? He did not believe so. It might be indiscreet, but there was nothing in it that revealed his location or the nature of his work.

He sealed the envelope, but put no name or address on it. Then he did something that was, strictly speaking, a direct violation of his oath. He enclosed the letter in another envelope which he addressed, with a covering note, to his lawyer in Washington. "Dear George," he wrote, "You'll be surprised to see where I am now. Jeannette doesn't know, and I don't want her to worry. So please address the enclosed to her and post it in the nearest mailbox. *Treat my present location as absolutely confidential.* I'll explain it all one day."

George would guess the truth, but he could keep secrets just as well as anyone in Central Intelligence. Sadler could think of no other fool-proof way of getting his letter to Jeannette, and he was prepared to take the slight risk for his peace of mind— and for hers.

He asked the way to the nearest mailbox (they were hard to find in Central City) and slid the letter down the chute. In a couple of hours it would be on the way to Earth; by this time tomorrow, it would have reached Jeannette. He could only hope that she would understand—or, if she could not understand, would suspend judgment until they met again.

There was a paper rack beside the mailbox, and Sadler purchased a copy of the *Central News.* He still had several hours before the monorail left for the Observatory, and if anything interesting was going on in town the local paper would presumably tell him all about it.

The political news received such little space that Sadler wondered if a mild censorship was in force. No one would have

40

realized that there was a crisis if he went by the headlines alone; it was necessary to search through the paper to find the really significant items. Low down on page two, for example, was a report that a liner from Earth was having quarantine trouble off Mars and was not being allowed to land—while another on Venus was not being allowed to take off. Sadler was fairly sure that the real trouble was political rather than medical; the Federation was simply getting tough.

On page four was a still more thought-provoking piece of news. A party of prospectors had been arrested on some remote asteroid in the vicinity of Jupiter. The charge, it seemed, was a violation of space-safety regulations. Sadler suspected that the charge was phony—and that so were the prospectors. Central Intelligence had probably lost some of its agents.

On the center page of the paper was a rather naive editorial making light of the situation and expressing the confident hope that common sense would prevail. Sadler, who had no illusions about the commonness of common sense, remained skeptical and turned to the local news.

All human communities, wherever they may be in space, follow the same pattern. People were getting born, being cremated (with careful conservation of phosphorus and nitrates), rushing in and out of marriage, moving out of town, suing their neighbors, having parties, holding protest meetings, getting involved in astonishing accidents, writing Letters to the Editor, changing jobs. . . . Yes, it was just like Earth. That was a somewhat depressing thought. Why had Man ever bothered to leave his own world if all his travels and experiences had made so little difference to his fundamental nature? He might just as well have stayed at home, instead of exporting himself and his foibles, at great expense, to another world.

Your job's making you cynical, Sadler told himself. Let's see what Central City has in the way of entertainment.

He'd just missed a tennis tournament in Dome Four, which should have been worth watching. It was played, so someone had told him, with a ball of normal size and mass. But the ball was honeycombed with holes, which increased its air-resistance so much that ranges were no greater than on earth. Without some such subterfuge, a good drive would easily span one of the

41

domes. However, the trajectories followed by these doctored balls were most peculiar, and enough to induce a swift nervous breakdown in anyone who had learned to play under normal gravity.

There was a cyclorama in Dome Three, promising a tour of the Amazon Basin (mosquito bites optional), starting at every alternate hour. Having just come from Earth, Sadler felt no desire to return so promptly. Besides, he felt he had already seen an excellent cyclorama display in the thunderstorm that had now passed out of sight. Presumably it had been produced in the same manner, by batteries of wide-angle projectors.

The attraction that finally took his fancy was the swimming pool in Dome Two. It was the star feature of the Central City gymnasium, much frequented by the Observatory staff. One of the occupational risks of life on the Moon was lack of exercise and resultant muscular atrophy. Anyone who stayed away from Earth for more than a few weeks felt the change of weight very severely when he came home. What lured Sadler to the gym, however, was the thought that he could practice some fancy dives that he would never dare risk on Earth, where one fell five meters in the first second and acquired far too much kinetic energy before hitting the water.

Dome Two was on the other side of the city, and as Sadler felt he should save his energy for his destination he took the subway. But he missed the slow-speed section which led one off the continuously moving belt, and was carried willy-nilly on to Dome Three before he could escape. Rather than circle the city again, he retraced the way on the surface, passing through the short connecting tunnel that linked all the domes together at the points where they touched. There were automatic doors here that opened at a touch—and would seal instantly if air-pressure dropped on either side.

Half the Observatory staff seemed to be exercising itself in the gym. Dr. Molton was sculling a rowing machine, one eye fixed anxiously on the indicator that was adding up his strokes. The chief engineer, eyes closed tightly as per the warning instructions, was standing in the center of a ring of ultra-violet tubes which gave out an eerie glare as they replenished his tan. One of the M.D.'s from Surgery was attacking a punchbag with such viciousness that Sadler hoped he would never have to meet him professionally. A tough-looking character who Sadler believed came from Maintenance was trying to see if he could lift a clear ton; even if one allowed mentally for the low gravity, it was still awe-inspiring to watch.

Everybody else was in the swimming pool, and Sadler quickly joined them. He was not sure what he had expected, but somehow he had imagined that swimming on the Moon would differ drastically from the same experience on the Earth. But it was exactly the same, and the only effect of gravity was the abnormal height of the waves, and the slowness with which they moved across the pool.

The diving went well as long as Sadler attempted nothing ambitious. It was wonderful to know just what was going on, and to have time to admire the surroundings during one's leisurely descent. Then, greatly daring, Sadler tried a somersault from five meters. After all, this was equivalent to less than a meter on Earth. . . .

Unfortunately, he completely misjudged his time of fall, and made half a turn too many—or too few. He landed on his shoulders, and remembered too late just what a crack one could give oneself even from a low height if things went wrong. Limping slightly, and feeling that he had been flayed alive, he crawled out of the pool. As the slow ripples ebbed languidly away, Sadler decided to leave this sort of exhibitionism to younger men.

After all this exertion, it was inevitable that he join Molton and a few of his other acquaintances when they left the gymnasium. Tired but relaxed, and feeling that he had learned a good deal more about the lunar way of life, Sadler leaned back in his seat as the monocab pulled out of the station and the great doors sealed tight behind them. Blue, cloud-flecked skies gave place to the harsh reality of the lunar night. There was the unchanged Earth, just as he had seen it hours ago. He looked for the blinding star of *Nova Draconis*, then remembered that in these latitudes it was hidden below the northern edge of the Moon.

The dark domes, which gave so little sign of the life and light they held, sank beneath the horizon. As he watched them go,

Sadler was struck by a sudden, somber thought. They had been built to withstand the forces that Nature could bring against them—but how pitiably fragile they would be if ever they faced the fury of Man!

Chapter VII

"I STILL THINK," said Jamieson, as the tractor headed toward the southern wall of Plato, "that there'll be a hell of a row when the Old Man hears about it."

"Why should he?" asked Wheeler. "When he gets back, he'll be too busy to bother about us. And anyway, we're paying for all the fuel we use. So stop worrying and enjoy yourself. This is our day off, in case you'd forgotten."

Jamieson did not reply. He was too busy concentrating on the road ahead—if it could be called a road. The only sign that other vehicles had ever been this way were the occasional furrows in the dust. Since these would last for eternity here on the windless Moon, no other signposts were needed, though occasionally one came across unsettling notices that read DANGER —CLEFTS AHEAD! or EMERGENCY OXYGEN—10 KILOMETERS.

There are only two methods of long-range transport on the Moon. The highspeed monorails link the main settlements with a fast, comfortable service running on a regular schedule. But the rail system is very limited, and likely to remain so because of its cost. For unrestricted ranging over the lunar surface, one must fall back on the powerful turbine-driven tractors known as "Caterpillars" or, more briefly, "Cats." They are, virtually, small spaceships mounted on fat little tires that enable them to go anywhere within reason even over the appallingly jagged surface of the Moon. On smooth terrain they can easily do a hundred kilometers an hour, but normally they are lucky to manage half that speed. The weak gravity, and the caterpillar treads they can lower if necessary, enable them to climb fantastic slopes. In emergencies, they have been known to haul themselves up vertical cliffs with their built-in winches. One can live in the larger models for weeks at a time without undue hardship, and all the detailed exploration of the Moon has been carried out by prospectors using these tough little vehicles.

Jamieson was a more-than-expert driver, and knew the way perfectly. Nevertheless, for the first hour Wheeler felt that his hair would never lie down again. It usually took newcomers to the Moon quite a while to realize that slopes of one-in-one were perfectly safe if treated with respect. Perhaps it was just as well that Wheeler was a novice, for Jamieson's technique was so unorthodox that it would have filled a more experienced passenger with real alarm.

Why Jamieson was such a recklessly brilliant driver was a paradox that had caused much discussion among his colleagues. Normally he was very painstaking and cautious, inclined not to act at all unless he could be certain of the consequences. No one had ever seen him really annoyed or excited; many thought him lazy, but that was a libel. He would spend weeks working on some observations until the results were absolutely unchallengeable—and would then put them away for two or three months to have another look at them later.

Yet once at the controls of a "cat," this quiet and peace-loving astronomer became a daredevil driver who held the unofficial record for almost every tractor run in the northern hemisphere. The reason lay—buried too deeply even for Jamieson to be aware of it himself—in a boyhood desire to be a spaceship pilot, a dream that had been frustrated by an erratic heart.

From space—or through a telescope on Earth—the walls of Plato seem a formidable barrier when the slanting sunlight shows them to best advantage. But in reality they are less than a kilometer high, and if one chooses the correct route through the numerous passes, the journey out of the crater and into the *Mare Imbrium* presents no great difficulty. Jamieson got through the mountains in less than an hour, though Wheeler wished that he had taken a little longer.

They came to a halt on a high escarpment overlooking the plain. Directly ahead, notching the horizon, was the pyramidal summit of Pico. Toward the right, sinking down into the northeast, were the more rugged peaks of the Teneriffe Mountains. Very few of those peaks had ever been climbed, largely because no one had so far bothered to attempt it. The brilliant Earth-light made them appear an uncanny blue-green, contrasting strangely with their appearance by day, when they would be bleached into raw whites and blacks by the merciless sun.

While Jamieson relaxed to enjoy the view, Wheeler began a careful search of the landscape with a pair of powerful binoculars. Ten minutes later he gave it up, having discovered nothing in the least unusual. He was not surprised by this, for the area where the unscheduled rockets had been landing was well below the horizon.

"Let's drive on," he said. "We can get to Pico in a couple of hours, and we'll have dinner there."

"And then what?" asked Jamieson in resigned tones.

"If we can't see anything, we'll come back like good little boys."

"O.K.—but you'll find it rough going from now on. I don't suppose more than a dozen tractors have ever been down there before. To cheer you up, I might tell you that our Ferdinand is one of them."

He eased the vehicle forward, gingerly skirting a vast talus slope where splintered rock had been accumulating for millennia. Such slopes were extremely dangerous, for the slightest disturbance could often set them moving in slow, irresistible avalanches that would overwhelm everything before them. For all his apparent recklessness, Jamieson took no real risks, and always gave such traps a very wide berth. A less experienced driver would have gaily galloped along the foot of the slide without a moment's thought—and ninety-nine times out of a hundred would have got away with it. Jamieson had seen what happened on the hundredth time. Once the wave of dusty rubble had engulfed a tractor, there was no escape, since any attempt at rescue would only start fresh slides.

Wheeler began to feel distinctly unhappy on the way down the outer ramparts of Plato. This was odd, for they were much less steep than the inner walls, and he had expected a smoother journey. He had not allowed for the fact that Jamieson would take advantage of the easier conditions to crowd on speed, with the result that Ferdinand was indulging in a peculiar rocking motion. Presently Wheeler disappeared to the rear of the well-

46

appointed tractor, and was not seen by his pilot for some time. When he returned he remarked rather crossly, "No one ever told me you could actually be seasick on the Moon."

The view was now rather disappointing, as it usually is when one descends to the lunar lowlands. The horizon is so near—only two or three kilometers away—that it gives a sense of confinement and restraint. It is almost as if the small circle of rock surrounding one is all that exists. The illusion can be so strong that men have been known to drive more slowly than necessary, as if subconsciously afraid they might fall off the edge of that uncannily near horizon.

For two hours Jamieson drove steadily onward, until at last the triple tower of Pico dominated the sky ahead. Once this magnificent mountain had been part of a vast crater wall that must have been a twin to Plato. But ages ago the encroaching lava of the *Mare Imbrium* had washed away all the rest of the hundred-and-fifty-kilometer-diameter ring, leaving Pico in lonely and solitary state.

The travelers paused here to open a few food packs and make some coffee in the pressure kettle. One of the minor discomforts of life on the Moon is that really hot drinks are an impossibility —water boils at about seventy degrees centigrade in the oxygen-rich, low-pressure atmosphere universally employed. After a while, however, one grows used to lukewarm beverages.

When they had cleared up the debris of the meal, Jamieson remarked to his colleague, "Sure you still want to go through with it?"

"As long as you say it's safe. Those walls look awfully steep from here."

"It's safe, if you do what I tell you. I was just wondering how you felt now. There's nothing worse than being sick in a spacesuit."

"*I'm* all right," Wheeler replied with dignity. Then another thought struck him. "How long will we be outside, anyway?"

"Oh, say a couple of hours. Four at the most. Better do all the scratching you want to now."

"I wasn't worrying about *that*," retorted Wheeler, and retired to the back of the cabin again.

In the six months he had been on the Moon, Wheeler had

47

worn a suit no more than a dozen times, and most of those occasions were on emergency drill. There were very few times when the observing staff had to go into vacuum—most of their equipment was remotely controlled. But he was not a complete novice, though he was still in the cautious stage which is so much safer than lighthearted overconfidence.

They called Base, *via* Earth, to report their position and intentions, then adjusted each other's equipment. First Jamieson, then Wheeler, chanted the alphabetical mnemonic—"A is for airlines, B is for batteries, C is for couplings, D is for D.F. loop . . ." which sounds so childish the first time one hears it, but which so quickly becomes part of the routine of lunar life—and is something nobody ever jokes about. When they were sure that all their equipment was in perfect condition, they cracked the doors of the airlock and stepped out onto the dusty plain.

Like most lunar mountains, Pico was not so formidable when seen close at hand as when glimpsed from a distance. There were a few vertical cliffs, but they could always be avoided, and it was seldom necessary to climb slopes of more than forty-five degrees. Under a sixth of a gravity, this is no great hardship, even when one is wearing a spacesuit.

Nevertheless, the unaccustomed exertion made Wheeler sweat and pant somewhat after they had been climbing for half an hour, and his face plate was misting badly so that he had to peer out of the corners to see properly. Though he was too stubborn to request a slower pace, he was very glad when Jamieson called a halt.

They were now almost a kilometer above the plain, and could see for at least fifty kilometers to the north. They shielded their eyes from the glare of the Earth and began to search.

It took only a moment to find their objective. Halfway to the horizon, two extremely large freight rockets were standing like ungainly spiders on their extended undercarriages. Large though they were, they were dwarfed by the curious dome-shaped structure rising out of the level plain. This was no ordinary pressure dome—its proportions were all wrong. It looked almost as if a complete sphere had been partly buried, so that the upper three-quarters emerged from the surface. Through his

48

binoculars, whose special eye pieces allowed him to use them despite his face plate, Wheeler could see men and machines moving round the base of the dome. From time to time clouds of dust shot into the sky and fell back again as if blasting was in progress. That was another odd thing about the Moon, he thought. Most objects fell too slowly here in this low gravity, for anyone accustomed to conditions on Earth. But dust fell much *too* quickly—at the same rate as anything else, in fact—for there was no air to check its descent.

"Well," said Jamieson after he too had carried out a long scrutiny through the glasses, "someone's spending an awful lot of money."

"What do you think it is? A mine?"

"It could be," replied the other, cautious as ever. "Perhaps they've decided to process the ores on the spot, and all their extraction plant is in that dome. But that's only a guess—I've certainly never seen anything like it before."

"We can reach it in an hour, whatever it is. Shall we go over and have a closer look?"

"I was afraid you were going to say that. I'm not sure it would be a very wise thing. They might insist on us staying."

"You've been reading too many scare articles. Anyone would think there was a war on and we were a couple of spies. They couldn't detain us—the Observatory knows where we are and the director would raise hell if we didn't get back."

"I suspect he will when we *do*, so we might as well get hung for sheep as lambs. Come along—it's easier on the way down."

"I never said it was hard on the way up," protested Wheeler, not very convincingly. A few minutes later, as he followed Jamieson down the slope, an alarming thought struck him.

"Do you think they're listening to us? Suppose someone's got a watch on this frequency—they'll have heard every word we've said. After all, we're in direct line of sight."

"Who's being melodramatic now? No one except the Observatory would be listening on this frequency, and the folks at home can't hear us as there's rather a lot of mountain in the way. Sounds as if you've got a guilty conscience; anyone would think that you'd been using naughty words again."

This was a reference to an unfortunate episode soon after

Wheeler's arrival. Since then he had been very conscious of the fact that privacy of speech, which is taken for granted on Earth, is not always available to the wearers of spacesuits, whose every whisper can be heard by anyone within radio range.

The horizon contracted about them as they descended to ground level, but they had taken careful bearings and knew which way to steer when they were back in Ferdinand. Jamieson was driving with extra caution now, for this was terrain over which he had never previously traveled. It was nearly two hours before the enigmatic dome began to bulge above the skyline, followed a little later by the squat cylinders of the freighters.

Once again, Wheeler aimed their roof antenna on Earth, and called the Observatory to explain what they had discovered and what they intended to do. He rang off before anyone could tell them not to do it, reflecting how crazy it was to send a message 800,000 kilometers in order to talk to someone a hundred kilometers away. But there was no other way of getting long-distance communication from ground level; everything below the horizon was blocked off by the shielding effect of the Moon. It was true that by using long waves it was sometimes possible to send signals over great distances by reflection from the Moon's very tenuous ionosphere, but this method was too unreliable to be of serious use. For all practical purposes, lunar radio contact had to be on a "line of sight" basis.

It was very amusing to watch the commotion that their arrival had caused. Wheeler thought it resembled nothing so much as an ant heap that had been well stirred with a stick. In a very short time they found themselves surrounded by tractors, moon-dozers, hauling machines, and excited men in spacesuits. They were forced by sheer congestion to bring Ferdinand to a halt.

"At any moment," said Wheeler, "they'll call out the guards."

Jamieson failed to be amused.

"You shouldn't make jokes like that," he chided. "They're apt to be too near the truth."

"Well, here comes the reception committee. Can you read the lettering on his helmet? SEC. 2, isn't it? 'Section Two,' I suppose that means."

"Perhaps. But SEC. could just as easily stand for Security. Well—it was all your idea. I'm merely the driver."

50

At that moment there was a series of peremptory knocks on the outer door of the airlock. Jamieson pressed the button that opened the seal and a moment later the "reception committee" was removing his helmet in the cabin. He was a grizzled, sharp-featured man with a worried expression that looked as though it was permanently built in. It did not appear that he was pleased to see them.

He regarded Wheeler and Jamieson thoughtfully, while the two astronomers put on their friendliest smiles. "We don't usu-ally get visitors in these parts," he said. "How did you happen to get here?"

The first sentence, Wheeler thought, was as good an under-statement as he had heard for some time.

"It's our day off—we're from the Observatory. This is Dr. Jamieson—I'm Wheeler. Astrophysicists, both of us. We knew you were around here, so decided to come and have a look."

"How did you know?" the other asked sharply. He still had not introduced himself, which would have been bad manners even on Earth and was quite shocking here.

"As you may have heard," said Wheeler mildly, "we possess one or two rather large telescopes over at the Observatory. And you've been causing us a lot of trouble. I, personally, have had two spectrograms ruined by rocket glare. So can you blame us for being a trifle inquisitive?"

A slight smile played around their interrogator's lips, and was instantly banished. Nevertheless, the atmosphere seemed to thaw a little.

"Well, I think it would be best if you come along to the office while we make a few checks. It won't take very long."

"I beg your pardon? Since when has any part of the Moon been private property?"

"Sorry, but that's the way it is. Come along, please."

The two astronomers climbed into their suits and followed through the airlock. Despite his aggressive innocence, Wheeler was beginning to feel a trifle worried. Already he was visualiz-ing all sorts of unpleasant possibilities; and recollections of what he had read about spies, solitary confinement and brick walls at dawn rose up to comfort him.

They were led to a smoothly fitting door in the curve of the great dome, and found themselves inside the space formed by the outer wall and an inner, concentric hemisphere. The two shells, as far as could be seen, were spaced apart by an intricate webbing of some transparent plastic. Even the floor underfoot was made of the same substance. This, Wheeler decided, was all very odd, but he had no time to examine it closely.

Their uncommunicative guide hurried them along almost at a trot, as if he did not wish them to see more than necessary. They entered the inner dome through a second airlock, where they removed their suits. Wheeler wondered glumly when they would be allowed to retrieve them again.

The length of the airlock indicated that the inner dome must be of tremendous thickness, and when the door ahead of them opened, both astronomers immediately noticed a familiar smell. It was ozone. Somewhere, not very far away, was high-voltage electrical equipment. There was nothing unduly remarkable about that, but it was another fact to be filed away for future reference.

The airlock had opened into a small corridor flanked by doors bearing painted numbers and such labels as PRIVATE, TECHNICAL STAFF ONLY, INFORMATION, STANDBY AIR, EMERGENCY POWER and CENTRAL CONTROL. Neither Wheeler nor Jamieson could deduce much from these notices, but they looked at each other thoughtfully when they were finally halted at a door marked SECURITY. Jamieson's expression told Wheeler, as clearly as any words could do "I told you so!"

After a short pause a "Come In" panel glowed and the door swung automatically open. Ahead lay a perfectly ordinary office dominated by a determined-looking man at a very large desk. The size of the desk was itself a proclamation to the world that money was no object here, and the astronomers contrasted it ruefully with the office equipment to which they were accustomed. A teleprinter of unusually complicated design stood on a table in one corner, and the remaining walls were entirely covered by file cabinets.

"Well," said the security officer, "who are these people?"

"Two astronomers from the Observatory over in Plato. They've just dropped in by tractor, and I thought you should see them."

"Most certainly. Your names, please?"

There followed a tedious quarter of an hour while particulars were carefully noted down and the Observatory was called. That meant, Wheeler thought glumly, that the fat would now be in the fire. Their friends in Signals, who had been logging their progress in case of any accident, would now have to report their absence officially.

At last their identities were established, and the man at the imposing desk regarded them with some perplexity. Presently his brows cleared and he began to address them.

"You realize, of course, that you are something of a nuisance. This is the last place we ever expected visitors, otherwise we'd have put up notices telling them to keep off. Needless to say, we have means of detecting any who may turn up, even if they're not sensible enough to drive up openly, as you did.

"However, here you are and I suppose there's no harm done. You have probably guessed that this is a government project, and one we don't want talked about. I'll have to send you back, but I want you to do two things."

"What are they?" asked Jamieson suspiciously.

"I want you to promise not to talk about this visit more than you have to. Your friends will know where you've gone, so you can't keep it a complete secret. Just don't discuss it with them, that's all."

"Very well," agreed Jamieson. "And the second point?"

"If anyone persists in questioning you, and shows particular interest in this little adventure of yours—report it at once. That's all. I hope you have a good ride home."

Back in the tractor, five minutes later, Wheeler was still fuming.

"Of all the high-handed so-and-sos! He never even offered us a smoke."

"I rather think," said Jamieson mildly, "that we were lucky to get off so easily. They meant business."

"I'd like to know what *sort* of business. Does that look like a mine to you? And why should anything be going on in a slag-heap like the *Mare?*"

"I think it must be a mine. When we drove up, I noticed something that looked very much like drilling machinery on

53

the other side of the dome. But it's hard to account for all the cloak-and-dagger nonsense."

"Unless they've discovered something that they don't want the Federation to know about."

"In that case we're not likely to find out, either, and might as well stop racking our brains. But to get on to more practical matters—where do we go from here?"

"Let's stick to our original plan. It may be some time before we have a chance of using Ferdy again, and we might as well make the most of it. Besides, it's always been one of my ambitions to see the *Sinus Iridum* from ground level, as it were."

"It's a good three hundred kilometers east of here."

"Yes, but you said yourself it was pretty flat, if we keep away from the mountains. We should be able to manage it in five hours. I'm a good-enough driver now to relieve you when you want a rest."

"Not over fresh ground—that would be far too risky. But we'll make a compromise. I'll take you as far as the Laplace Promontory, so that you'll have a look into the Bay. And then you can drive home, following the track I've made. Mind you stick to it, too."

Wheeler accepted gladly. He had been half afraid that Jamieson would abandon the trip and sneak back to the Observatory, but decided that he had done his friend an injustice.

For the next three hours they crawled along the flanks of the Teneriffe Mountains, then struck out across the plain to the Straight Range, that lonely, isolated band of mountains like a faint echo of the mighty Alps. Jamieson drove now with a steady concentration; he was going into new territory and could take no chances. From time to time he pointed out famous landmarks and Wheeler checked them against the photographic chart.

They stopped for a meal about ten kilometers east of the Straight Range, and investigated more of the boxes which the Observatory kitchen had given them. One corner of the tractor was fitted out as a tiny galley, but they didn't intend to do any real cooking except in an emergency. Neither Wheeler nor Jamieson was a sufficiently good cook to enjoy the preparation of meals and this, after all, *was* a holiday. . . .

"Sid," began Wheeler abruptly, between mouthfuls of sandwich, "what do you think about the Federation? You've met more of their people than I have."

"Yes, and liked them. Pity you weren't here before the last crowd left; we had about a dozen of them at the Observatory studying the telescope mounting. They're thinking of building a fifteen-hundred-centimeter instrument on one of the moons of Saturn, you know."

"That would be quite a project—I always said we're too close to the sun here. It would certainly get clear of the Zodiacal Light and the other rubbish around the inner planets. But to get back to the argument—did they strike you as likely to start a quarrel with Earth?"

"It's difficult to say. They were very open and friendly with us, but then we were all scientists together and that helps a lot. It might have been different if we'd been politicians or civil servants."

"Dammit, we *are* civil servants! That fellow Sadler was reminding me of it only the other day."

"Yes, but at least we're *scientific* civil servants, which makes quite a difference. I could tell that they didn't care a lot for Earth, though they were too polite to say so. There's no doubt that they're annoyed about the metals allocations; I often heard them complain about it. Their main point is that they have much greater difficulties than we have, in opening up the outer planets, and that Earth wastes half the stuff she uses."

"Which side do you think is right?"

"I don't know; it's so hard to get at all the facts. But there are a lot of people on Earth who are afraid of the Federation and don't want to give it any more power. The Federals know that; one day they may grab first and argue afterward."

Jamieson screwed up the wrappings and tossed them into the waste bin. He glanced at the chronometer, then swung himself up into the driving seat. "Time to get moving again," he said. "We're falling behind schedule."

From the Straight Range they swung southeast, and presently the great headland of Promontory Laplace appeared on the skyline. As they rounded it, they came across a disconcerting sight—the battered wreck of a tractor, and beside it a rough cairn surmounted by a metal cross. The tractor seemed to have been destroyed by an explosion in its fuel tanks, and was an obsolete model of a type that Wheeler had never seen before. He was not surprised when Jamieson told him it had been there for almost a century; it would still look exactly the same a million years from now.

As they rolled past the headland, the mighty northern wall of the *Sinus Iridum*—the Bay of Rainbows—swept into view. Eons ago the *Sinus Iridum* had been a complete ring mountain—one of the largest walled-plains on the Moon. But the cataclysm which had formed the Sea of Rains had destroyed the whole of the southern wall, so that only a semicircular bay is now left. Across that bay Promontory Laplace and Promontory Heraclides stare at each other, dreaming of the day when they were linked by mountains four kilometers high. Of those lost mountains, all that now remain are a few ridges and low hillocks.

Wheeler was very quiet as the tractor rolled past the great cliffs, which stood like a line of titans full-face toward the Earth. The green light splashing down their flanks revealed every detail of the terraced walls. No one had ever climbed those heights, but one day, Wheeler knew, men would stand upon their summits and stare out in victory across the Bay. It was strange to think that after two hundred years, there was so much of the Moon untrodden by human feet, and so many places that a man must reach with nothing to aid him but his own exertions and skill.

He remembered his first glimpse of the *Sinus Iridum*, through the little homemade telescope he had built when he was a boy. It had been nothing more than two small lenses fixed in a cardboard tube, but it had given him more pleasure than the giant instruments of which he was now the master.

Jamieson swung the tractor round in a great curve, and brought it to a halt facing back toward the west. The line they had trampled through the dust was clearly visible, a road which would remain here forever unless later traffic obliterated it.

"The end of the line," he said. "You can take over from here. She's all yours until we get to Plato. Then wake me up and I'll take her through the mountains. Good night."

56

How he managed it, Wheeler couldn't imagine, but within ten minutes Jamieson was asleep. Perhaps the gentle rocking of the tractor acted as a lullaby, and he wondered how successful he would be in avoiding jolts and jars on the way home. Well, there was only one way to find out. . . . He aimed carefully at the dusty track, and began to retrace the road to Plato.

Chapter VIII

IT WAS BOUND TO HAPPEN sooner or later, Sadler told himself philosophically, as he knocked at the director's door. He had done his best, but in work like this it was impossible to avoid hurting someone's feelings. It would be interesting, very interesting, to know who had complained. . . .

Professor Maclaurin was one of the smallest men Sadler had ever seen. He was so tiny that some people had made the fatal mistake of not taking him seriously. Sadler knew better than this. Very small men usually took care to compensate for their physical deficiencies (how many dictators had been of even average height?) and from all accounts Maclaurin was one of the toughest characters on the Moon.

He glared at Sadler across the virgin, uncluttered surface of his desk. There was not even a scribbling pad to break its bleakness—only the small panel of the communicator switchboard with its built-in speaker. Sadler had heard about Maclaurin's unique methods of administration, and his hatred of notes and memoranda. The Observatory was run, in its day-to-day affairs, almost entirely by word of mouth. Of course, other people had to prepare notices and schedules and reports— Maclaurin just switched on his mike and gave the orders. The system worked flawlessly for the simple reason that the director recorded everything, and could play it back at a moment's notice to anyone who said, "But, sir, you never told me *that*!" It was rumored—though Sadler suspected this was a libel—that Maclaurin had occasionally committed verbal forgery by retrospectively altering the record. Such a charge, needless to say, was virtually impossible to prove.

The director waved to the only other seat, and started talking before Sadler could reach it.

"I don't know whose brilliant idea this was," he began, "but I was never notified that you were coming here. If I had been, I would have asked for a postponement. Although no one appreciates the importance of efficiency more than I do, these are very troubled times. It seems to me that my men could be better employed than by explaining their work to you—particularly while we are coping with the *N. Draconis* observations."

"I'm sorry there was a failure to inform you, Professor Maclaurin," Sadler replied. "I can only assume that the arrangements were made while you were en route to Earth." He wondered what the director would think if he knew how carefully matters had been arranged in this precise manner. "I realize that I must be something of a nuisance to your staff, but they have given me every assistance and I've had no complaints. In fact, I thought I was getting on rather well with them."

Maclaurin rubbed his chin thoughtfully. Sadler stared in fascination at the tiny, perfectly formed hands, no larger than those of a child.

"How much longer do you expect to be here?" the director asked. He certainly doesn't worry about your feelings, Sadler told himself wryly.

"It's very hard to say—the area of my investigation is so undefined. And it's only fair to warn you that I've scarcely started on the scientific side of your work, which is likely to present the greatest difficulties. So far I have confined myself to Administration and Technical Services."

This news did not seem to please Maclaurin. He looked like a small volcano working up to an eruption. There was only one thing to do, and Sadler did it quickly.

He walked to the door, opened it swiftly, looked out, then closed it again. This piece of calculated melodrama held the director speechless while Sadler walked over to the desk and brusquely flicked down the switch on the communicator.

"Now we can talk," he began. "I wanted to avoid this, but I see it's inevitable. Probably you've never met one of these cards before."

The still flabbergasted director, who had probably never

before in his life been treated like this, stared at the blank sheet of plastic. As he watched, a photograph of Sadler, accompanied by some lettering, flashed into view—then vanished abruptly.

"And what," he asked when he had recovered his breath, "is Central Intelligence? I've never heard of it."

"You're not supposed to," Sadler replied. "It's relatively new, and highly unadvertised. I'm afraid the work I'm doing here is not exactly what it seems. To be brutally frank, I could hardly care less about the efficiency of your establishment, and I completely agree with all the people who tell me that it's nonsense to put scientific research on a cost-accounting basis. But it's a plausible story, don't you think?"

"Go on," said Maclaurin, with dangerous calm.

Sadler was beginning to enjoy himself beyond the call of duty. It wouldn't do, however, to get drunk with power. . . .

"I'm looking for a spy," he said, with a bleak and simple directness.

"Are you serious? This is the twenty-second century!"

"I am perfectly serious, and I need not impress upon you that you must reveal nothing of this conversation to anybody, even Wagnall."

"I refuse to believe," snorted Maclaurin, "that any of my staff would be engaged in espionage. The idea's fantastic."

"It always is," Sadler replied patiently. "That doesn't alter the position."

"Assuming that there's the slightest basis in this charge, have you any idea who it might be?"

"If I had, I'm afraid I couldn't tell you at this stage. But I'll be perfectly frank. We're not certain that it is anyone here—we're merely acting on a nebulous hint one of our—ah—agents picked up. But there is a leak *somewhere* on the Moon, and I'm covering this particular possibility. Now you see why I have been so inquisitive. I've tried not to act out of character, and I think that by now I'm taken for granted by everybody. I can only hope that our elusive Mr. X, if he exists at all, has accepted me at my face value. This, by the way, is why I'd like to know who has been complaining to you. I assume that somebody has."

Maclaurin hummed and hawed for a moment, then capitulated.

"Jenkins, down in Stores, rather implied that you'd been taking up a lot of his time."

"That's very interesting," said Sadler, more than a little puzzled. Jenkins, chief storekeeper, had been nowhere near his list of suspects. "As a matter of fact, I've spent relatively little time there—just enough to make my mission look convincing. I'll have to keep an eye on Mr. Jenkins."

"This whole idea is all very new to me," said Maclaurin thoughtfully. "But even if we have someone here passing out information to the Federation, I don't quite see how they would do it. Unless it was one of the signals officers, of course."

"That's the key problem," admitted Sadler. He was willing to discuss the general aspects of the case, for the director might be able to throw some light on them. Sadler was all too aware of his difficulties, and the magnitude of the task he had been set. As a counterspy, his status was strictly amateur. The only consolation he had was that his hypothetical opponent would be in the same position. Professional spies had never been too numerous in any age, and the last one must have died more than a century ago.

"By the way," said Maclaurin, with a forced and somewhat unconvincing laugh. "How do you know that *I'm* not the spy?"

"I don't," Sadler replied cheerfully. "In counter-espionage, certainty is rare. But we do the best we can. I hope you weren't seriously inconvenienced during your visit to Earth?"

Maclaurin stared uncomprehendingly at him for a moment. Then his jaw dropped.

"So you've been investigating *me*!" he spluttered indignantly.

Sadler shrugged his shoulders.

"It happens to the best of us. If it's any consolation, you can just imagine what *I* had to go through before they gave me this job. And I never asked for it in the first place. . . ."

"Then what do you want me to do?" growled Maclaurin. For a man of his size, his voice was surprisingly deep, though Sadler had been told that when he was really annoyed it developed a high-pitched squeak.

"Naturally, I'd like you to inform me of anything suspicious that comes to your notice. From time to time I may consult you on various points, and I'd be very glad of your advice. Otherwise, please take as little notice of me as possible and continue to regard me as a nuisance."

"*That*," replied Maclaurin, with a half-hearted smile, "will present no difficulties at all. However, you can count on me to assist you in every way—if only to help prove that your suspicions are unfounded."

"I sincerely hope that they are," Sadler replied. "And thank you for your co-operation—I appreciate it."

Just in time, he stopped himself whistling as he closed the door behind him. He felt very pleased that the interview had gone so well, but he remembered that no one whistled after they had had an interview with the director. Adjusting his expression to one of grave composure, he walked out through Wagnall's office and into the main corridor, where he at once ran into Jamieson and Wheeler.

"Have you seen the Old Man?" Wheeler asked anxiously. "Is he in a good mood?"

"As this is the first time I've met him, I've no standards of reference. We got on well enough. What's the matter? You look like a couple of naughty schoolboys."

"He's just asked for us," said Jamieson. "We don't know why, but he's probably been catching up on what's happened while he's away. He's already congratulated Con for discovering *N. Draconis,* so it can't be that. I'm afraid he's found out that we've borrowed a Cat for a run."

"What's wrong with that?"

"Well, they're only supposed to be used on official jobs. But everybody does it—as long as we replace the fuel we burn, no one's any the worse. Heck, I suppose I shouldn't have told that to *you*, of all people!"

Sadler did a quick double-take, then realized with relief that Jamieson was merely referring to his well-advertised activities as a financial watchdog.

"Don't worry," he laughed. "The worst I'll do with the information is to blackmail you into taking me for a ride. I hope the Old Ma—Professor Maclaurin—doesn't give you too rough a passage."

All three would have been quite surprised to know with what uncertainty the director himself was regarding this interview. In the ordinary way, such minor infractions of the rules as unauthorized used of a Caterpillar would have been a matter for Wagnall to deal with, but something more important was involved here. Until five minutes ago, he had no idea what it might be, and had asked to see Wheeler and Jamieson to discover what was going on. Professor Maclaurin prided himself on keeping in touch with everything, and a certain amount of his staff's time and ingenuity had to be employed in seeing that he was not always successful.

Wheeler, drawing heavily on the stock of good will *N. Draconis* had given him, gave an account of their unofficial mission. He tried to make it sound as if they were a pair of knights in armor riding out into the wilderness to discover the dragon which was menacing the Observatory. He concealed nothing of importance, which was well for him as the director already knew where he had been.

As he listened to Wheeler's account, Maclaurin found the pieces of the jigsaw fitting together. This mysterious message from Earth, ordering him to keep his people out of the *Mare Imbrium* in future, must have originated from the place these two had visited. The leak that Sadler was investigating would also have something to do with it. Maclaurin still found it hard to believe that any of his men was a spy, but he realized that a spy was the last thing any competent spy ever looked like.

He dismissed Jamieson and Wheeler with an absent-minded mildness that left them both sorely puzzled. For a moment he sat lost in gloomy thought. It might be a coincidence, of course —the story hung together well. But if one of these men was after information, he had set about it in the right way. Or had he? Would a real spy have acted so openly, knowing that he was bound to draw suspicion on himself? Could it even be a daring double-bluff, on the principle that no one would seriously suspect such a frontal attack?

Thank God, it wasn't his problem. He would get it off his hands as quickly as he could. Professor Maclaurin snapped down the TRANSMIT switch and spoke to the outer office.

"Please find Mr. Sadler for me. I want to speak to him again."

Chapter IX

THERE HAD BEEN a subtle change in Sadler's status since the director's return. It was something that Sadler had known must happen, though he had done his best to guard against it. On his arrival, he had been treated with polite suspicion by everybody, and it had taken him several days solid public-relations work to break down the barriers. People had become friendly and talkative, and he could make some headway. But now they seemed to be regretting their earlier frankness, and it was uphill work once more.

He knew the reason. Certainly no one suspected his real purpose in being here, but everybody knew that the return of the director, far from limiting his activities, had somehow enhanced his position. In the echoing sounding-box of the Observatory, where rumor and gossip traveled at speeds scarcely inferior to that of light, it was hard to keep any secrets. The word must have gone out that Sadler was more important than he seemed. He only hoped it would be a long while before anybody guessed *how* much more important. . . .

Until now, he had confined his attention to the Administrative section. This was partly a matter of policy, because this would be the way he would be expected to act. But the Observatory really existed for the scientists, not the cooks, typists, accountants and secretaries, however essential they might be.

If there was a spy in the Observatory, there were two main problems he had to face. Information is useless to a spy unless he can send it to his superiors. Mr. X must not only have contacts who passed material to him—he must have an out-going channel of communication as well.

Physically, there were only three ways out of the Observatory. One could leave it by monorail, by tractor, or on foot. The last case did not seem very likely to be important. In theory, a man might walk a few kilometers and leave a message to be picked up at some prearranged rendezvous. But such peculiar behavior would soon be noticed, and it would be very easy to check on the small number of men in Maintenance who were the only people who used suits regularly. Every exit and entrance through the airlocks had to be logged, though Sadler doubted that this rule was invariably obeyed.

The tractors were more promising, as they would give so much greater range. But their use would involve collusion, since they always carried a crew of at least two men—and this was one rule which was *never* broken, for safety reasons. There was the odd case of Jamieson and Wheeler, of course. Their backgrounds were being busily investigated now, and he should have the report in a few days. But their behavior, though irregular, had been too open to be really suspicious.

That left the monorail to Central City. Everybody went there, on the average, about once a week. There were endless possibilities for the exchange of messages here, and at this very moment a number of "tourists" were inconspicuously checking contacts and making all sorts of interesting discoveries about the private lives of the Observatory staff. There was little part that Sadler could play in this work, except to furnish lists of the most frequent visitors to the City.

So much for physical lines of communication. Sadler discounted them all. There were other, and subtler, means far more likely to be used by a scientist. Any member of the Observatory's staff could build a radio transmitter, and there were countless places where one could be concealed. It was true that the patiently listening monitors had detected nothing, but sooner or later Mr. X would make a slip.

Meanwhile, Sadler would have to find what the scientists were doing. The high-pressure course in astronomy and physics he had taken before coming here would be totally inadequate to give him any real understanding of the Observatory's work, but at least he would be able to get the general outline. And he might eliminate a few suspects from his depressingly long list.

The Computing Section did not detain him for long. Behind their glass panels, the spotless machines sat in silent cogitation while the girls fed the program tapes into their insatiable maws. In an adjacent sound-proofed room, the electric typewriters stormed away, printing endless rows and columns of numbers. Dr. Mays, the head of the section, did his best to explain what was going on—but it was a hopeless task. These machines had left far behind such elementary operations as integration, such kindergarten functions as cosines or logarithms. They were dealing with mathematical entities of which Sadler had never heard, and solving problems whose very statement would be meaningless to him.

That did not worry him unduly; he had seen what he wanted to. All the main equipment was sealed and locked; only the maintenance engineers who called once a month could get at it. Certainly there was nothing for him here. Sadler tiptoed away as from a shrine.

The optical workshop, where patient craftsmen shaped glass to a fraction of a millionth of an inch, using a technique unchanged for centuries, fascinated him but advanced his search no further. He peered at the interference fringes produced by clashing light waves, and watched them scurry madly back and forth as the heat of his body caused microscopic expansions in blocks of flawless glass. Here art and science met, to achieve perfections unmatched elsewhere in the whole range of human technology. Could there be any clue for him here in this buried factory of lenses, prisms and mirrors? It seemed most improbable.

He was, Sadler thought glumly, rather in the position of a man in a darkened coal cellar, looking for a black cat that might not be there. What was worse, to make the analogy more accurate he would have to be a man who didn't know what a cat looked like, even when he saw one.

His private discussions with Maclaurin helped him a good deal. The director was still skeptical, but was obviously cooperating to the full if only to get this annoying interloper out of the way. Sadler could question him about any technical aspect of the Observatory's work, though he was careful not to give any hints as to the direction his search was taking him.

He had now compiled a small dossier for every member of the staff—no mean achievement, even though the factual data had been supplied before he came to the Observatory. For most of his subjects, a single sheet of paper sufficed, but for some he had accumulated several pages of cryptic notes. The facts he was sure of he wrote in ink; the speculations were in pencil so that they could be modified when necessary. Some of these speculations were very wild and frequently libelous, and Sadler often felt very ashamed of them. It was hard, for example, to accept a drink from someone whom you had noted down as possibly susceptible to bribes owing to the cost of maintaining an expensive mistress in Central City. . . .

This particular suspect had been one of the engineers in Construction. Sadler had soon ruled him out as a likely candidate for blackmail, since far from concealing the situation the victim was always complaining bitterly about his inamorata's extravagances. He had even warned Sadler against incurring similar liabilities.

The filing system was divided into three parts. Section A contained the names of the ten or so men Sadler considered the most probable suspects, though there was not one against whom he had any real evidence. Some were down simply because they had the greatest opportunity for passing out information if they wished to do so. Wagnall was one of these; Sadler was practically certain that the secretary was innocent, but kept him on the list to be on the safe side.

Several others were listed because they had close relatives in the Federation, or because they were too openly critical of Earth. Sadler did not really imagine that a well-trained spy would risk arousing suspicion by behaving in this way, but he had to be on the watch for the enthusiastic amateur who could be just as dangerous. The records of atomic espionage during the Second World War had been very instructive in this respect, and Sadler had studied them with great care.

Another name on List A was that of Jenkins, the chief store-keeper. This was only the most tenuous of hunches, and all attempts by Sadler to follow it up had been unsuccessful. Jenkins seemed to be a somewhat morose individual, who resented interference and was not very popular with the rest of the staff. Getting anything out of him in the way of equipment was supposed to be the most difficult job on the Moon. This, of course, might merely mean that he was a good representative of his proverbially tenacious tribe.

66

There remained that interesting couple Jamieson and Wheeler, who between them did a great deal to enliven the Observatory scene. Their drive out into the *Mare Imbrium* had been a fairly typical exploit, and had followed, so Sadler was assured, the pattern of earlier adventures.

Wheeler was always the leading spirit. His trouble—if it was a trouble—was that he had too much energy and too many interests. He was not yet thirty; one day, perhaps, age and responsibility would mellow him, but so far neither had had much opportunity. It was too easy to dismiss him as a case of arrested development, as a college boy who had failed to grow up. He had a first-rate mind, and never did anything that was really foolish. Though there were many people who did not like him, particularly after they had been the victims of one of his practical jokes, there was nobody who wished him any harm. He moved unscathed through the little jungle of Observatory politics, and had the abiding virtues of complete honesty and forthrightness. One always knew what he was thinking, and it was never necessary to ask him for his opinion. He gave it first.

Jamieson was a very different character, and presumably it was the contrast in their personalities which drew these two men together. He was older than Wheeler by a couple of years, and was regarded as a sobering influence on his younger companion. Sadler doubted this; as far as he could judge, Jamieson's presence had never made any difference in his friend's behavior. He had mentioned this to Wagnall, who had thought for a while and said, "Yes, but think how much worse Con would be if Sid *wasn't* there to keep an eye on him."

Certainly Jamieson was far more stable and much harder to get to know. He was not as brilliant as Wheeler and would probably never make any shattering discoveries, but he would be one of those reliable, sound men who do the essential tidying up after the geniuses have broken through into new territory.

Scientifically reliable—yes. Politically reliable—that was another matter. Sadler had tried to sound him, without making it too obvious, but so far with little success. Jamieson seemed more interested in his work and his hobby—the painting of lunar landscapes—than in politics. During his term at the

Observatory he had built up a small art gallery, and whenever he had the chance he would go out in a spacesuit carrying easel and special paints made from low-vapor-pressure oils. It had taken him a good deal of experimenting to find pigments that could be used in a vacuum, and Sadler frankly doubted that the results were worth the trouble. He thought he knew enough about art to decide that Jamieson had more enthusiasm than talent, and Wheeler shared this point of view. "They say that Sid's pictures grow on you after a while," he had confided to Sadler. "Personally, I can think of no more horrible fate."

Sadler's List B contained the names of everybody else in the Observatory who looked intelligent enough to be a spy. It was depressingly long, and from time to time he went through it trying to transfer people to List A or—better still—to the third and final list of those who were completely clear of suspicion. As he sat in his little cubicle, shuffling his sheets and trying to put himself into the places of the men he was watching, Sadler sometimes felt that he was playing an intricate game, in which most of the rules were flexible and all the players unknown. It was a deadly game, the moves were taking place at accelerating speed—and upon its outcome might depend the future of the human race.

Chapter X

THE VOICE that came from the speaker was deep, cultured and sincere. It had been traveling across space for many minutes, beamed through the clouds of Venus along the two-hundred-million-kilometer link to Earth, then relayed again from Earth to Moon. After that immense journey, it was still clear and clean, almost untouched by interference or distortion.

"The situation here has hardened since my last commentary. No one in official circles will express any opinion, but the press and radio are not so reticent. I flew in from Hesperus this morning, and the three hours I've been here are quite long enough for me to gauge public opinion.

"I must speak bluntly, even if I have to upset the people

back home. Earth isn't very popular here. The phrase 'dog in the manger' gets bandied around quite a lot. Your own supply difficulties are recognized, but it's felt that the frontier planets are short of necessities while Earth wastes much of its resources on trivial luxuries. I'll give you an example. Yesterday the news came in that the Mercury outpost has just lost five men through a faulty heat-exchange unit in one of the domes. The temperature control failed and the lava got them —not a very nice death. If the manufacturer had not been short of titanium, this wouldn't have happened.

"Of course, it's not fair to blame Earth for this. But it's unfortunate that only a week ago you cut the titanium quota again, and the interested parties here are seeing that the public doesn't forget it. I can't be more specific than that, because I don't want to be cut off, but you'll know who I mean.

"I don't believe that the situation will get any worse unless some new factor enters the picture. But suppose—and here I want to make it quite clear that I'm only considering a hypothetical case—suppose Earth were to locate new supplies of the heavy metals. In the still-unexplored ocean depths, for instance. Or even on the Moon, despite the disappointments it's given in the past.

"If this happens, and Earth tries to keep its discovery to itself, the consequences may be serious. It's all very well to say that Earth would be within its rights. Legal arguments don't carry much weight when you're fighting thousand-atmosphere pressures on Jupiter, or trying to thaw out the frozen moons of Saturn. Don't forget, as you enjoy your mild spring days and peaceful summer evenings, how lucky you are to live in the temperate region of the solar system, where the air never freezes and the rocks never melt. . . .

"What is the Federation likely to do if such a situation arises? If I knew, I couldn't tell you. I can only make some guesses. To talk about war, in the old-fashioned sense, seems absurd to me. Either side could inflict heavy damage on the other, but any real trial of strength could not possibly be conclusive. Earth has too many resources, even though they are dangerously concentrated. And she owns most of the ships in the solar system.

69

"The Federation has the advantage of dispersion. How can Earth carry out a simultaneous fight against half-a-dozen planets and moons, poorly equipped though they may be? The supply problem would be completely hopeless.

"If, which heaven forbid, it should come to violence, we may see sudden raids on strategic points by specially equipped vessels which will make an attack and then retreat into space. Any talk of interplanetary invasion is pure fantasy. Earth certainly has no wish to take over the planets. And the Federation, even if it wanted to enforce its will on Earth, has neither the men nor the ships for a full-scale assault. As I see it, the immediate danger is that something like a duel may take place —where and how is anyone's guess—as one side attempts to impress the other with its strength. But I would warn any who may be thinking of a limited, gentlemanly war that wars were seldom limited, and never gentlemanly. Good-by, Earth—this is Roderick Beynon, speaking to you from Venus."

Someone reached out and turned off the set, but at first nobody seemed inclined to start the inevitable discussion. Then Jansen, from Power, said admiringly:

"Beynon's got guts, you must admit. He wasn't pulling his punches. I'm surprised they let him make that broadcast."

"I thought he talked good sense," remarked Mays. The High Priest of Computing had a slow, measured style of delivery that contrasted quaintly with the lightning speed of his machines.

"Whose side are you on?" someone asked suspiciously.

"Oh, I'm a friendly neutral."

"But Earth pays your salary. Which side would you support if there was a showdown?"

"Well that would depend on the circumstances. I'd *like* to support Earth. But I reserve the right to make up my own mind. Whoever it was who said 'My planet right or wrong' was a damned fool. I'd be for Earth if it was right, and would probably give it the benefit of the doubt in a borderline case. But I'd not support it if I felt its cause was definitely wrong."

There was a long silence while everyone thought this over. Sadler had been watching Mays intently while the mathematician was speaking. Everyone, he knew, respected Mays's honesty and logic. A man who was actively working against Earth would never have expressed himself as forthrightly as this. Sadler wondered if Mays would have spoken any differently had he known that a counter-intelligence man was sitting within two meters of him. He did not believe that he would have altered a word.

"But, blast it," said the chief engineer, who as usual was blocking the synthetic fire, "there's no question of right and wrong here. Anything found on Earth or Moon belongs to us, to do with as we like."

"Certainly, but don't forget we've been falling back on our quota deliveries, as Beynon said. The Federation has been relying on them for its programs. If we repudiate our agreements because we haven't got the stuff ourselves, that's one thing. But it's a very different matter if we *have* got it and are just holding the Federation up for ransom."

"Why should we do any such thing?"

It was Jamieson, unexpectedly enough, who answered this. "Fear," he said. "Our politicians are frightened of the Federation. They know it already has more brains, and one day it may have more power. Then Earth will be a back number."

Before anyone could challenge him on this, Czuikov from the Electronics Lab started a fresh hare.

"I've been thinking," he said, "about that broadcast we've just heard. We know that Beynon's a pretty honest man, but after all he was broadcasting from Venus, with their permission. There may be more in that talk of his than meets the ear."

"What do you mean?"

"He may be putting across their propaganda. Not consciously, perhaps; they may have primed him to say what they want us to hear. That talk about raids, for instance. Perhaps it's intended to scare us."

"That's an interesting idea. What do you think, Sadler? You're the last to come up from Earth."

This frontal attack took Sadler rather by surprise, but he dexterously tossed the ball back.

"I don't think Earth can be frightened as easily as that. But the passage that interested me was his reference to pos-

71

sible new supplies on the Moon. It looks as if rumors are beginning to float around."

This was a calculated indiscretion on Sadler's part. It was not so very indiscreet, however, for there was no one in the Observatory who did not know (a) that Wheeler and Jamieson had stumbled on some unusual government project in the *Mare Imbrium,* and (b) that they had been ordered not to talk about it. Sadler was particularly anxious to see what their reactions would be.

Jamieson assumed a look of puzzled innocence, but Wheeler did not hesitate to rise to the bait.

"What do you expect?" he said. "Half the Moon must have seen those ships coming down in the *Mare.* And there must be hundreds of workmen there. They can't all have come from Earth—they'll be going into Central City and talking to their girl friends when they've had a few drinks too many."

How right you are, thought Sadler, and what a headache *that* little problem was giving Security. . . .

"Anyway," continued Wheeler, "I've got an open mind on the subject. They can do what they like out there as long as they don't interfere with me. You can't tell a thing from the outside of the place, except that it's costing the poor taxpayer an awful lot of money."

There was a nervous cough from a mild little man from Instrumentation, where only that morning Sadler had spent a boring couple of hours looking at cosmic-ray telescopes, magnetometers, seismographs, molecular-resonance clocks, and batteries of other devices which were surely storing information more rapidly than anyone would ever be able to analyze it.

"I don't know about them interfering with you, but they've been playing hell with me."

"What do you mean?" everyone asked simultaneously.

"I had a look at the magnetic-field-strength meters half an hour ago. Usually the field here is pretty constant, except when there's a storm around, and we always know when to expect those. But something odd's going on at the moment. The field keeps hopping up and down—not very much, a few microgauss—and I'm sure it's artificial. I've checked all the equipment in the Observatory, and everyone swears they're not mucking around with magnets. I wondered if our secretive friends out in the *Mare* were responsible, and just on the chance, I had a look at the other instruments. I didn't find anything until I came to the seismographs. We've got a telemetering one down by the south wall of the crater, you know, and it had been knocked all over the place. Some of the kinks looked like blasting; I'm always picking that up from Hyginus and the other mines. But there were also some most peculiar jitters of the trace that were almost synchronized with the magnetic pulses. Allowing for the time-lag through the rock, the distance checked up well. There's no doubt where it comes from."

"An interesting piece of research," Jamieson remarked, "but what does it add up to?"

"There are probably a good many interpretations. But I'd say that out there in the *Mare Imbrium* someone is generating a colossal magnetic field, in pulses lasting about a second at a time."

"And the moon-quakes?"

"Just a by-product. There's a lot of magnetic rock around here, and I imagine it must get quite a jolt when that field goes on. You probably wouldn't notice that quake even if you were where it started, but our seismographs are so sensitive they can spot a meteor falling twenty kilometers away."

Sadler listened to the resulting technical argument with great interest. With so many keen minds worrying around the facts, it was inevitable that some would guess the truth—and inevitable that others would counter it with their own theories. This was not important; what concerned him was whether anyone showed special knowledge or curiosity.

But no one did, and Sadler was still left with his discouraging three propositions: Mr. X was too clever for him; Mr. X was not here; Mr. X did not exist at all. . . .

Chapter XI

NOVA DRACONIS was waning; no longer did it outshine all the suns of the Galaxy. Yet in the skies of Earth it was still

73

brighter than Venus at her most brilliant, and it might be a thousand years before men saw its like again.

Though it was very near on the scale of stellar distances, *N. Draconis* was still so remote that its apparent magnitude did not vary across the whole width of the solar system. It shone with equal brilliance above the firelands of Mercury and the nitrogen glaciers of Pluto. Transient though it was, it had turned men's minds for a moment from their own affairs and made them think of ultimate realities.

But not for long. The fierce violet light of the greatest nova in history shone now upon a divided system, upon planets that had ceased to threaten each other and were now preparing for deeds.

The preparations were far more advanced than the public realized. Neither Earth nor the Federation had been frank with its people. In secret laboratories, men had been turning toward destruction the tools which had given them the freedom of space. Even if the contestants had worked in entire independence, it was inevitable that they would have evolved similar weapons, since they were basing them on the same technologies.

But each side had its agents and counter-agents, and each knew, at least approximately, the weapons which the other was developing. There might be some surprises—any one of which could be decisive—but on the whole the antagonists were equally matched.

In one respect, the Federation had a great advantage. It could hide its activities, its researches and tests, among the scattered moons and asteroids, beyond any hope of discovery. Earth, on the other hand, could not launch a single ship without the information reaching Mars and Venus within a matter of minutes.

The great uncertainty that plagued each side was the effiency of its Intelligence. If this came to war, it would be a war of amateurs. A secret service requires a long tradition, though perhaps not an honorable one. Spies cannot be trained overnight, and even if they could, the kind of flair that characterizes a really brilliant agent is not easy to come by.

No one was better aware of this than Sadler. Sometimes he

wondered if his unknown colleagues, scattered over the solar system, felt equally frustrated. Only the man at the top could see the complete picture—or something approaching it. He had never realized the isolation in which a spy must work, the horrible feeling that you are alone, that there is no one you can trust, no one with whom you can share your burdens. Since he had reached the Moon, he had—at least to his knowledge —spoken to no other member of Central Intelligence. All his contacts with the organization had been impersonal and indirect. His routine reports—which to any casual reader would have seemed extremely dull analyses of the Observatory's accounts—went by the daily monorail to Central City, and he had little idea what happened to them after that. A few messages had arrived by the same means, and in the event of real emergency the teleprinter circuit was available.

He was looking forward to his first meeting with another agent, which had been arranged weeks in advance. Though he doubted if it would be of much practical value, it would give his morale a badly needed boost.

Sadler had not, to his own satisfaction at least, acquainted himself with all the main aspects of Administration and Technical Services. He had looked (from a respectful distance) into the burning heart of the micro-pile which was the Observatory's main power source. He had watched the big mirrors of the solar generators, waiting patiently for the sunrise. They had not been used for years, but it was nice to have them around in case of any emergency, ready to tap the limitless resources of the sun itself.

The Observatory farm had surprised and fascinated him most of all. It was strange that in this age of scientific marvels, of synthetic this and artificial that, there were still some things in which Nature could not be excelled. The farm was an integral part of the air-conditioning system, and was at its best during the long lunar day. When Sadler saw it, lines of fluorescent lamps were providing substitute sunlight, and metal shutters had been drawn over the great windows which would greet the dawn when the sun rose above the western wall of Plato.

He might have been back on Earth, in some well-appointed

greenhouse. The slowly moving air passed along the rows of growing plants, gave up its carbon dioxide and emerged not only richer in oxygen, but also with that indefinable freshness which the chemists had never been able to duplicate.

And here Sadler was presented with a small but very ripe apple, every atom of which had come from the Moon. He took it back to his room where he could enjoy it in privacy, and was no longer surprised that the farm was out of bounds to everyone except the men who tended it. The trees would soon be stripped if any casual visitor could wander through these verdant corridors.

The Signals section was just about as great a contrast as could be imagined. Here were the circuits that linked the Observatory with Earth, with the rest of the Moon, and if necessary with the planets direct. It was the greatest and most obvious danger point. Every message that came or went was monitored, and the men who operated the equipment had been checked and rechecked by Security. Two of the staff had been transferred, without knowing the reason, to less sensitive jobs. Moreover—even Sadler did not know this—a telescopic camera thirty kilometers away was taking a photograph every minute of the big transmitting arrays which the Observatory used for long-distance work. If one of these radio searchlights happened to point for any length of time in an unauthorized direction, the fact would soon be known.

The astronomers, without exception, were all very willing to discuss their work and explain their equipment. If they wondered at some of Sadler's questions, they gave no sign of it. For his part, he was very careful not to step outside of his adopted role. The technique he used was the frank man-to-man one: "Of course this isn't really my job, but I'm quite interested in astronomy, and while I'm here on the Moon I went to see all I can. Naturally, if you're too busy at the moment——" It always worked like a charm.

Wagnall usually made the arrangements and smoothed the way for him. The secretary had been so helpful that at first Sadler wondered if he was trying to safeguard himself, but further inquiry had shown that Wagnall was like that. He was one of those people who cannot help trying to create a good impression, simply because they want to be on good terms with everybody. He must find it singularly frustrating, Sadler thought, working for a cold fish like Professor Maclaurin.

The heart of the Observatory was, of course, the thousand-centimeter telescope—the largest optical instrument ever made by man. It stood on the summit of a slight knoll some distance from the residential area and was impressive rather than elegant. The enormous barrel was surrounded by a gantry-like structure which controlled its vertical movement, and the whole framework could rotate on a circular track.

"It's not a bit like any of the telescopes back on Earth," explained Molton as they stood together inside the nearest observation dome, looking out across the plain. "The tube, for instance. That's so we can still work during the day. Without it, we'd get sunlight reflected down into the mirror from the supporting structure. That would ruin our observations, and the heat would distort the mirror. It might take hours to settle down again. The big reflectors on Earth haven't got to worry about this sort of thing. They're only used at night—those that are still in action at all."

"I wasn't sure that there were any active observatories left on Earth," Sadler remarked.

"Oh, there are a few. Nearly all training establishments, of course. *Real* astronomical research is impossible down in that pea-soup of an atmosphere. Look at my own work, for instance —ultra-violet spectroscopy. The Earth's atmosphere is *completely* opaque to the wavelengths I'm interested in. No one ever observed them until we got out into space. Sometimes I wonder how astronomy ever *started* down on Earth."

"The mounting looks odd to me," Sadler remarked thoughtfully, "It's more like that of a gun than any telescope I've ever seen."

"Quite correct. They didn't bother about an equatorial mounting. There's an automatic computer that keeps it tracking any star we set it on. But come downstairs and see what happens at the business end."

Molton's laboratory was a fantastic maze of half-assembled equipment, scarcely any of which Sadler could recognize. When he complained about this, his guide seemed highly amused.

"You needn't feel ashamed of that. We've designed and built most of it here; we're always trying out improvements. But roughly speaking, what happens is this. The light from the big mirror—we're directly underneath it here—is piped down through that tube over there. I can't demonstrate at the moment, as someone is taking photographs and it's not my turn for another hour. But when it is, I can select any part of the sky I like from this remote-control desk here and lock the instrument on to it. Then all I have to do is to analyze the light with these spectroscopes. You can't see much of their works, I'm afraid—they're all totally enclosed. When they're in use the whole optical system has to be evaluated, because as I mentioned just now even a trace of air blocks the far ultra-violet rays."

Sadler was suddenly struck by an incongruous thought.

"Tell me," he said, glancing round the maze of wiring, the batteries of electronic counters, the atlases of spectral lines, "have you ever *looked* through this telescope?"

Molton smiled back at him.

"Never," he said. "It wouldn't be hard to arrange, but there would be absolutely no point in it. All these really big telescopes are super-cameras. And who wants to look through a camera?"

There were, however, telescopes at the Observatory through which one could look without too much trouble. Some of the smaller instruments were fitted with TV cameras which could be swung into position when it was necessary to search for comets or asteroids whose exact locations were unknown. Once or twice Sadler managed to borrow one of these instruments, and to sweep the skies at random to see what he could find. He would dial a position on the remote-control board, then peer into the screen to see what he had caught. After a while he discovered how to use the *Astronautical Almanac*, and it was a great moment when he set up the co-ordinates for Mars and found it bang in the middle of the field.

He stared with mixed feelings at the green-and-ocher disk almost filling the screen. One of the polar caps was tilted slightly sunward—it was the beginning of spring, and the great frost-covered tundras would be slowly thawing after the iron winter. A beautiful planet to watch from space, but a hard planet on which to build a civilization. No wonder its sturdy children were losing patience with Earth.

The image of the planet was incredibly sharp and clear. There was not the slightest tremor or unsteadiness as it floated in the field of view, and Sadler, who had once glimpsed Mars through a telescope on Earth, could now see with his own eyes how astronomy had been liberated from its chains when the atmosphere had been left behind. Earth-bound observers had studied Mars for decades through instruments larger than this, but he could see more in a few hours than they could have glimpsed in a lifetime. He was no nearer to Mars than they had been—indeed, the planet was now at a considerable distance from Earth—but there was no dancing, quivering haze of air to veil his view.

When he had gazed his fill at Mars, he searched for Saturn. The sheer beauty of the spectacle took his breath away: it seemed impossible that he was not looking at some perfect work of art, rather than a creation of nature. The great yellow globe, slightly flattened at the poles, floated at the center of its intricate system of rings. The faint bands and shadings of atmospheric disturbances were clearly visible, even across two thousand million kilometers of space. And beyond the concentric girdles of the rings, Sadler could count at least seven of the planet's moons.

Though he knew that the instantaneously operating eye of the television camera could never rival the patient photographic plate, he also looked for some of the distant nebulae and star clusters. He let the field of view drift along the crowded highway of the Milky Way, checking the image whenever some particularly beautiful group of stars, or cloud of glowing mist appeared upon the screen. After a while, it seemed to Sadler that he had become intoxicated with the infinite splendor of the skies; he needed something that would bring him back into the realm of human affairs. So he turned the telescope on Earth.

It was so huge that even under the weakest power he could get only part of it on the screen. The great crescent was shrinking fast, but even the unlit portion of the disk was full of interest. Down there in the night were the countless phosphorescent glows that marked the positions of cities—and down there was Jeannette, sleeping now, but perhaps dreaming of him. At least he knew that she had received his letter; her puzzled but guarded reply had been reassuring, though its loneliness and unspoken reproach had torn at his heart. Had he, after all, made a mistake? Sometimes he bitterly regretted the conventional caution which had ruled the first year of their married life. Like most couples on the overpopulated planet that swam before his eyes, they had waited to prove their compatibility before embarking on the adventure of parenthood. In this age, it was a definite social stigma to have children before one had been married for several years—it was a proof of fecklessness and irresponsibility.

They had both wanted a family, and now that such matters could be decided in advance had intended to start with a son. Then Sadler had received his assignment, and realized for the first time the full seriousness of the interplanetary situation. He would not bring Jonathan Peter into the uncertain future that lay ahead.

In earlier ages, few men would have hesitated for such a reason. Indeed, the possibility of their own extinction had often made them even more anxious to seek the only immortality human beings can know. But the world had been at peace for two hundred years, and if war came now the complex and fragile pattern of life on Earth might be broken into fragments. A woman burdened with a child might have little chance of survival.

Perhaps he was being melodramatic, and had let his fears overpower his sense of judgment. If Jeannette had known all the facts, she would still not have hesitated; she would have taken the chance. But because he could not talk to her freely, he would not take advantage of her ignorance.

It was too late for regret; all that he loved lay there on that sleeping globe, sundered from him by the abyss of space. His thoughts had come full circle. He had made the journey from star to man, across the immense desert of the Cosmos to the lonely oasis of the human soul.

Chapter XII

"I'VE NO REASON TO SUPPOSE," said the man in the blue suit, "that anyone suspects you, but it would be difficult to meet inconspicuously in Central City. There are too many people around, and everybody knows everybody else. You'd be surprised how hard it is to get any privacy."

"You don't think it will seem odd for me to come here?" asked Sadler.

"No, most visitors do, if they can manage it. It's like going to Niagara Falls—something no one wants to miss. You can't blame them, can you?"

Sadler agreed. Here was one spectacle that could never be a disappointment, that would always surpass any advance publicity. Even now the shock of stepping out onto this balcony had not completely worn off; he could well believe that many people were physically incapable of coming as far as this.

He was standing above nothingness, encased in a transparent cylinder jutting out from the edge of the canyon. The metal catwalk beneath his feet, and the slim hand rail, were the only tokens of security granted to him. His knuckles still grasped that railing tightly.

The Hyginus Cleft ranks among the greatest wonders on the Moon. From end to end it is more than three hundred kilometers long, and in places it is five kilometers wide. It is not so much a canyon as a series of interlinked craters, branching out in two arms from a vast central well. And it is the gateway through which men have reached the buried treasures of the Moon.

Sadler could now look down into the depths without flinching. Infinitely far below, it seemed, some strange insects were slowly crawling back and forth in little pools of artificial light. If one shone a torch upon a group of cockroaches, they would have looked like this.

But those tiny insects, Sadler knew, were the great mining machines at work on the floor of the canyon. It was surprisingly flat down there, so many thousands of meters below, for it seemed that lava had flooded into the cleft soon after it was formed, and then congealed into a buried river of rock.

The Earth, almost vertically overhead, illuminated the great wall immediately opposite. The canyon marched away to right and left as far as the eye could follow, and sometimes the blue-green light falling upon the rock face produced a most unexpected illusion. Sadler found it easy to imagine, if he moved his head suddenly, that he was looking into the heart of a gigantic waterfall, sweeping down forever into the depths of the Moon.

Across the face of that fall, on the invisible threads of hoisting cables, the ore buckets were rising and dropping. Sadler had seen those buckets, moving on the overhead lines away from the Cleft, and he knew that they were taller than he was. But now they looked like beads moving slowly along a wire, as they carried their loads to the distant smelting plants. It's a pity, he thought to himself, that they're only carrying sulphur and oxygen and silicon and aluminum—we could do with fewer of the light elements and more of the heavy ones.

But he had been called here on business, not to stand gaping like a tourist. He pulled the coded notes from his pocket, and began to give his report.

It did not take as long as he could have wished. There was no way of telling whether his listener was pleased or disappointed at the inconclusive summary. He thought it over for a minute, then remarked, "I wish we could give you some more help, but you can imagine how shorthanded we are now. Things are getting rough; if there is going to be trouble, we expect it in the next ten days. There's something happening out around Mars, but we don't know what it is. The Federation has been building at least two ships of unusual design, and we think they're testing them. Unfortunately we haven't a single sighting, only some rumors that don't make sense but have worried Defense. I'm telling you this to give you more background. No one here should know about it, and if you hear anybody talking on these lines it will mean that they've somehow had access to classified information.

"Now about your short list of provisional suspects. I see you've got Wagnall down, but he's clear with us."

"O.K. I'll move him to List B."

"Then Brown, Lefevre, Tolanski—they've certainly had no contacts here."

"Can you be sure of that?"

"Fairly. They use their off-duty hours here in highly non-political ways."

"I'd suspected that," Sadler remarked, permitting himself the luxury of a smile. "I'll take them off altogether."

"Now this man Jenkins, in Stores. Why are you so keen on keeping him?"

"I've no real evidence at all. But he seems about the only person who's taken any objection to my nominal activities."

"Well, we'll continue to watch him from this end. He comes to town quite often, but of course he's got a good excuse—he does most of the local purchasing. That leaves you with five names on your A list, doesn't it?"

"Yes, and frankly, I'll be very surprised if it's any of them. Wheeler and Jamieson we've already discussed. I know that Maclaurin's suspicious of Jamieson after that trip out to the *Mare Imbrium,* but I don't put much reliance on that. It was largely Wheeler's idea, anyway.

"Then there are Benson and Carlin. Their wives come from Mars, and they keep getting into arguments whenever the news is being discussed. Benson's an electrician in Tech Maintenance; Carlin's a medical orderly. You could say they have some motive, but it's a pretty tenuous one. Moreover, they'd be rather too obvious suspects."

"Well, here's another we'd like you to move up to your List A. This fellow Molton."

"Dr. Molton?" exclaimed Sadler in some surprise. "Any particular reason?"

"Nothing serious, but he's been to Mars several times on astronomical missions and has some friends there."

"He never talks politics. I've tackled him once or twice and he just didn't seem interested. I don't think he meets many people in Central City—he seems completely wrapped up in his work and I think he only goes into town to keep fit in the gym. You've nothing else?"

"No—sorry. It's still a fifty-fifty case. There's a leak *somewhere,* but it may be in Central City. The report about the

Observatory may be a deliberate plant. As you say, it's very hard to see how anyone there could pass on information. The radio monitors have detected nothing except a few unauthorized personal messages which were quite innocent."

Sadler closed his notebook and put it way with a sigh. He glanced once more down into the vertiginous depths above which he was so insecurely floating. The cockroaches were crawling briskly away from a spot at the base of the cliff, and suddenly a slow stain seemed to spread across the floodlit wall. (*How* far down was that? Two kilometers? Or three?) A puff of smoke emerged, and instantly dispersed into the vacuum. Sadler began to count the seconds to time his distance from the explosion, and had got to twelve before he remembered that he was wasting his efforts. If that had been an atom bomb, he would have heard nothing here.

The man in blue adjusted his camera strap, nodded at Sadler, and became the perfect tourist again.

"Give me ten minutes to get clear," he said, "and remember not to know me if we meet again."

Sadler rather resented that last advice. After all, he was not a complete amateur. He had been fully operational for almost half a lunar day.

Business was slack at the little café in the Hyginus station, and Sadler had the place to himself. The general uncertainty had discouraged tourists; any who happened to be on the Moon were hurrying home as fast as they could get shipping space. They were probably doing the right thing; if there was trouble, it would be here. No one really believed that the Federation would attack Earth directly and destroy millions of innocent lives. Such barbarities belong to the past—so it was hoped. But how could one be sure? Who knew what might happen if war broke out? Earth was so fearfully vulnerable.

For a moment Sadler lost himself in reveries of longing and self-pity. He wondered if Jeannette had guessed where he was. He was not sure, now, that he wanted her to know. It would only increase her worries.

Over his coffee—which he still ordered automatically though he had never met any on the Moon worth drinking—he considered the information his unknown contact had given to him. It had been of very little value; he was still groping in the dark. The tip about Molton was a distinct surprise, and he did not take it too seriously. There was a kind of trustworthiness about the astrophysicist which made it hard to think of him as a spy. Sadler knew perfectly well that it was fatal to rely on such hunches, and whatever his own feelings, he would now pay extra attention to Molton. But he made a private bet with himself that it would lead nowhere.

He marshaled all the facts he could remember about the head of the Spectroscopy Section. He already knew about Molton's three trips to Mars. The last visit had been over a year ago, and the director himself had been there more recently than that. Moreover, among the interplanetary brotherhood of astronomers, there was probably no member of the senior staff who did not have friends on both Mars and Venus.

Were there any unusual features about Molton? None that Sadler could think of, apart from that curious aloofness that seemed to conflict with a real inner warmth. There was, of course, his amusing and rather touching "flower-bed," as he had heard someone christen it. But if he was to start investigating innocent eccentricities like *that*, he'd never get anywhere.

There was one thing that might be worth looking into, however. He'd make a note of the shop where Molton purchased his replacements (it was almost the only place outside the gym he ever visited), and one of the counter-agents in the city could sniff around it. Feeling rather pleased with himself at thus proving he was missing no chances, Sadler paid his bill and walked up the short corridor connecting the café with the almost deserted station.

He rode the spur-line back to Central City, over the incredibly broken terrain past Triesnecker. For almost all the journey, the monorail track was accompanied by the pylons passing their loaded buckets out from Hyginus, and the empty ones back. The long cables, with their kilometer spans, were the cheapest and most practical means of conveyance—if there was no particular hurry to deliver the goods. Soon after the domes of Central City appeared on the skyline, however, they changed direction and curved off to the right. Sadler could see them marching away down to the horizon toward the great chemical plants which, directly or indirectly, fed and clothed every human being on the Moon.

He no longer felt a stranger in the city, and went from dome to dome with the assurance of a seasoned traveler. The first priority was an overdue haircut; one of the Observatory cooks earned some extra money as a barber, but having seen the results, Sadler preferred to stick to the professionals. Then there was just time to call at the gym for fifteen minutes in the centrifuge.

·As usual, the place was full of Observatory staff making sure they would be able to live on Earth again when they wished to. There was a waiting list for the centrifuge, so Sadler dumped his clothes in a locker and went for a swim until the descending whine of the motor told him that the big machine was ready for a new cargo of passengers. He noticed, with wry amusement, that two of his List-A suspects—Wheeler and Molton—and no less than seven of the Class-B ones were present. But it was not so surprising about Class B. Ninety per cent of the Observatory staff were on *that* unwieldly list, which if it had been titled at all would have been called: "Persons sufficiently intelligent and active to be spies, but concerning whom there is no evidence one way or the other."

The centrifuge held six people, and had some ingenious safety device which prevented its starting unless the load was properly balanced. It refused to co-operate until a fat man on Sadler's left had changed places with a thin man opposite; then the motor began to pick up speed and the big drum with its slightly anxious human cargo started to turn on its axis. As the speed increased, Sadler felt his weight steadily mounting. The direction of the vertical was shifting, too—it was swinging round toward the center of the drum. He breathed deeply, and tried to see if he could lift his arms. They felt as if they were made of lead.

The man on Sadler's right staggered to his feet and began to walk to and fro, keeping within the carefully defined white lines that marked the limits of his territory. Everyone else was doing the same; it was uncanny to watch them standing on what, from the point of view of the Moon, was a vertical surface. But they were glued to it by a force six times as great as the Moon's feeble gravity—a force equal to the weight they would have had on Earth.

It was not a pleasant sensation. Sadler found it almost impossible to believe that until a few days ago he had spent his entire existence in a gravity field of this strength. Presumably he would get used to it again, but at the moment it made him feel as weak as a kitten. He was heartily glad when the centrifuge slowed down and he was able to crawl back into the gentle gravity of the friendly Moon.

He was a tired and somewhat discouraged man as the monorail pulled out of Central City. Even the brief glimpse he caught of the new day, as the still-hidden sun touched the highest pinnacles of the western mountains, failed to cheer him. He had been here more than twelve days of Earth time, and the long lunar night was ending. But he dreaded to think what the day might bring.

Chapter XIII

EVERY MAN HAS HIS WEAKNESS, if you can find it. Jamieson's was so obvious that it seemed unfair to exploit it, but Sadler could not afford to have any scruples. Everyone in the Observatory regarded the young astronomer's painting as a subject for mild amusement, and gave him no encouragement at all. Sadler, feeling a considerable hypocrite, began to play the role of sympathetic admirer.

It had taken some time to break through Jamieson's reserve and to get him to speak frankly. The process could not be hurried without arousing suspicion, but Sadler had made fair progress by the simple technique of supporting Jamieson when his colleagues ganged up on him. This happened, on the average, every time he produced a new picture.

To steer the conversation from art to politics took less skill than might have been expected, for politics was never very far away these days. Yet oddly enough, it was Jamieson himself who raised the questions that Sadler had been trying to ask.

He had obviously been thinking hard, in his methodical way, wrestling with the problem that had concerned every scientist, to a greater and greater extent, since the day when atomic power was born on Earth.

"What would you do," he asked Sadler abruptly, a few hours after the latter's return from Central City, "if you had to chose between Earth and the Federation?"

"Why ask me?" replied Sadler, trying to conceal his interest.

"I've been asking a lot of people," Jamieson replied. There was a wistfulness in his voice, the puzzled wonder of someone looking for guidance in a strange and complex world. "Do you remember that argument we had in the Common Room, when Mays said that whoever believed in 'my planet, right or wrong' was a fool?"

"I remember," Sadler answered cautiously.

"I think Mays was right. Loyalty isn't just a matter of birth, but ideals. There can be times when morality and patriotism clash."

"What's started you philosophizing on these lines?"

Jamieson's reply was unexpected.

"*Nova Draconis*," he said. "We've just got in the reports from the Federation observatories out beyond Jupiter. They were routed through Mars, and someone there had attached a note to them—Molton showed it to me. It wasn't signed, and it was quite short. It merely said that *whatever* happened—and the word was repeated twice—they'd see that their reports continued to reach us."

A touching example of scientific solidarity, thought Sadler; it had obviously made a deep impression on Jamieson. Most men—certainly most men who were not scientists—would have thought the incident rather trivial. But trifles like this could sway men's minds at crucial moments.

"I don't know just what you deduce from this," said Sadler, feeling like a skater on very thin ice. "After all, everybody knows that the Federation has plenty of men who are just as honest and well-intentioned and co-operative as anyone here. But you can't run a solar system on gusts of emotion. Would you really hesitate if it came to a showdown between Earth and the Federation?"

There was a long pause. Then Jamieson sighed.

"I don't know," he answered. "I really don't know."

It was a completely frank and honest answer. As far as Sadler was concerned, it virtually eliminated Jamieson from his list of suspects.

The fantastic incident of the searchlight in the *Mare Imbrium* occurred nearly twenty-four hours later. Sadler heard about it when he joined Wagnall for morning coffee, as he usually did when he was near Administration.

"Here's something to make you think," said Wagnall as Sadler walked into the secretary's office. "One of the technicians from Electronics was up in the dome just now, admiring the view, when suddenly a beam of light shot up over the horizon. It lasted for about a second, and he says it was a brilliant blue-white. There's no doubt that it came from that place that Wheeler and Jamieson visited. I know that Instrumentation has been having trouble with them, and I've just checked. Their magnetometers were kicked right off scale ten minutes ago, and there's been a severe local 'quake.' "

"I don't see how a searchlight would do that sort of thing," answered Sadler, genuinely puzzled. Then the full implications of the statement reached him.

"A beam of light?" he gasped. "Why, that's impossible. It wouldn't be visible in the vacuum here."

"Exactly," said Wagnall, obviously enjoying the other's mystification. "You can only see a light beam when it passes through something. And this was really brilliant—almost dazzling. The phrase Williams used was 'it looked like a solid bar.' Do you know what *I* think that place is?"

"No," replied Sadler, wondering how near Wagnall had got to the truth. "I haven't any idea."

The secretary looked rather bashful, as if trying out a theory of which he was a little ashamed.

"I think it's some kind of fortress. Oh, I know it sounds fantastic, but when you think about it, you'll see it's the only explanation that fits all the facts."

Before Sadler could reply, or indeed think of a suitable answer, the desk buzzer sounded and a slip of paper dropped out of Wagnall's teleprinter. It was a standard Signals form, but there was one non-standard item about it. It carried the crimson banner of Priority.

Wagnall read it aloud, his eyes widening as he did so.

URGENT TO DIRECTOR PLATO OBSERVATORY
DISMANTLE ALL SURFACE INSTRUMENTS AND MOVE ALL DELICATE EQUIPMENT UNDERGROUND COMMENCING WITH LARGE MIRRORS. RAIL SERVICE SUSPENDED UNTIL FURTHER NOTICE. KEEP STAFF UNDERGROUND AS FAR AS POSSIBLE. EMPHASIZE THIS PRECAUTIONARY REPEAT PRECAUTIONARY MEASURE. NO IMMEDIATE DANGER EXPECTED.

"And that," said Wagnall slowly, "appears to be that. I'm very much afraid my guess was perfectly correct."

It was the first time that Sadler had ever seen the entire Observatory staff gathered together. Professor Maclaurin stood on the raised dais at the end of the main lounge—the traditional place for announcements, musical recitals, dramatic interludes and other forms of Observatory entertainment. But no one was being entertained now.

"I fully understand," said Maclaurin bitterly, "what this means to your programs. We can only hope that this move is totally unnecessary, and that we can start work again within a few days. But obviously we can take no chances with our equipment—the five-hundred and the thousand-centimeter mirrors must be got under cover at once. I have no idea what form of trouble is anticipated, but it seems we are in an unfortunate position here. If hostilities do break out, I shall signal at once to both Mars and Venus reminding them that this is a scientific institution, that many of their nationals have been honored guests here, and that we are of no conceivable military importance. Now please assemble behind your group leaders, and carry out your instructions as swiftly and efficiently as possible."

The director walked down from the dais. Small though he was, he seemed still more shrunken now. In that moment, there was no one in the room who did not share his feelings, however much they might have inveighed against him in the past.

90

"Is there anything I can do?" asked Sadler, who had been left out of the hastily drawn-up emergency plans.

"Ever worn a spacesuit?" said Wagnall.

"No, but I don't mind trying."

To Sadler's disappointment, the secretary shook his head firmly.

"Too dangerous—you might get in trouble and there aren't enough suits to go around, anyway. But I could do with some more help in the office—we've had to tear up all the existing programs and go over to a two-watch system. So all the rotas and schedules have to be rearranged—you could help on this."

That's what comes of volunteering for anything, thought Sadler. But Wagnall was right; there was nothing he could do to help the technical teams. As for his own mission, he could probably serve it better in the secretary's office than anywhere else, for it would be the operational headquarters from now on.

Not, thought Sadler grimly, that it now mattered a great deal. If Mr. X had ever existed, and was still in the Observatory, he could now relax with the consciousness of a job well done.

Some instruments, it had been decided, would have to take their chance. These were the smaller ones, which could be easily replaced. Operation Safeguard, as someone with a penchant for military nomenclature had christened it, was to concentrate on the priceless optical components of the giant telescopes and coelostats.

Jamieson and Wheeler drove out with Ferdinand and collected the mirrors of the interferometer, the great instrument whose twin eyes, twenty kilometers apart, made it possible to measure the diameters of the stars. The main activity, however, centered round the thousand-centimeter reflector.

Molton was in charge of the mirror team. The work would have been impossible without his detailed knowledge of the telescope's optical and engineering features. It would have been impossible, even with his help, if the mirror had been cast in a single unit, like that of the historic instrument that still stood atop Mount Palomar. This mirror, however, was built from more than a hundred hexagonal sections, dovetailed together

91

into a great mosaic. Each could be removed separately and carried to safety, though it was slow and tedious work and it would take weeks to reassemble the complete mirror with the fantastic precision needed.

Spacesuits are not really designed for this sort of work, and one helper, through inexperience or haste, managed to drop his end of a mirror section as he lifted it out of the cell. Before anyone could catch it, the big hexagon of fused quartz had picked up enough speed to chip off one of its corners. This was the only optical casualty, which in the circumstances was very creditable.

The last tired and disheartened men came in through the airlocks twelve hours after the operation had commenced. Only one research project continued—a single telescope was still following the slow decline of *Nova Draconis* as it sank toward final extinction. War or no war, this work would go on.

Soon after the announcement that the two big mirrors were safe, Sadler went up to one of the observation domes. He did not know when he would have another chance to see the stars and the waning Earth, and he wished to carry the memory down into his subterranean retreat.

As far as the eye could tell, the Observatory was quite unchanged. The great barrel of the thousand-centimeter reflector pointed straight to the zenith; it had been swung over to the vertical to bring the mirror cell down to ground level. Nothing short of a direct hit could damage this massive structure, and it would have to take its chances in the hours or days of danger that lay ahead.

There were still a few men moving around in the open; one of them, Sadler noticed, was the director. He was perhaps the only man on the Moon who could be recognized when wearing a spacesuit. It had been specially built for him, and brought his height up to a full meter and a half.

One of the open trucks used for moving equipment around the Observatory was scuttling across toward the telescope, throwing up little gouts of dust. It halted beside the great circular track on which the framework revolved, and the spacesuited figures clambered clumsily aboard. Then it made off briskly to the right, and disappeared into the ground as it descended the ramp leading into the airlocks of the garage.

The great plain was deserted, the Observatory blind save for the one faithful instrument pointing toward the north in sublime defiance of the follies of man. Then the speaker of the ubiquitous public-address system ordered Sadler out of the dome, and he went reluctantly into the depths. He wished he could have waited a little longer, for in a few more minutes the western walls of Plato would be touched by the first fingers of the lunar dawn. It seemed a pity that no one would be there to greet it.

Slowly the Moon was turning toward the sun, as it could never turn toward the Earth. The line of day was crawling across the mountains and plains, banishing the unimaginable cold of the long night. Already the entire westward wall of the Apennines was ablaze, and the *Mare Imbrium* was climbing into the dawn. But Plato still lay in darkness, lit only by the radiance of the waning Earth.

A group of scattered stars suddenly appeared low down in the western sky. The tallest spires of the great ring-wall were catching the sun, and minute by minute the light spread down their flanks, until it linked them together in a necklace of fire. Now the sun was striking clear across the whole vast circle of the crater, as the ramparts on the east lifted into the dawn. Any watchers down on Earth would see Plato as an unbroken ring of light, surrounding a pool of inky shadow. It would be hours yet before the rising sun could clear the mountains and subdue the last strongholds of the night.

There were no eyes to watch when, for the second time, that blue-white bar stabbed briefly at the southern sky. That was well for Earth. The Federation had learned much, but there were still some things which it might discover too late.

Chapter XIV

THE OBSERVATORY had settled down for a siege of indefinite duration. It was not, on the whole, as frustrating an experience as might have been expected. Although the main programs had been interrupted, there was endless work to do in reducing results, checking theories, and writing papers, which until now had been put aside for lack of time. Many of the astronomers almost welcomed the break, and several fundamental advances in cosmology were a direct outcome of this enforced idleness.

The worst aspect of the whole affair, everyone agreed, was the uncertainty and lack of news. What was really going on? Could one believe the bulletins from Earth, which seemed to be trying to soothe the public while at the same time preparing it for the worst?

As far as could be observed, some kind of attack was expected, and it was just the Observatory's bad luck that it was so near a possible danger point. Perhaps Earth guessed what form the attack would take, and certainly it had made some preparations to meet it.

The two great antagonists were circling each other, each unwilling to strike the first blow, each hoping to bluff the other into capitulation. But they had gone too far, and neither could retreat without a loss of prestige too damaging to be faced.

Sadler feared that the point of no return had already been passed. He was sure of it when the news came over the radio that the Federation Minister at the Hague had delivered a virtual ultimatum to the government of Earth. It charged Earth with failing to meet its agreed quotas of heavy metals, of deliberately withholding supplies for political purposes, and of concealing the existence of new resources. Unless Earth agreed to discuss the allocation of these new resources, she would find it impossible to use them herself.

The ultimatum was followed, six hours later, by a general broadcast to Earth, beamed from Mars by a transmitter of astonishing power. It assured the people of Earth that no harm would befall them, and that if any damage was done to the home planet it would be an unfortunate accident of war, for which their own government must take the blame. The Federation would avoid any acts which might endanger populated areas, and it trusted that its example would be followed.

The Observatory listened to this broadcast with mixed feelings. There was no doubt as to its meaning, and no doubt that the *Mare Imbrium* was, within the meaning of the Act, an

94

unpopulated area. One effect of the broadcast was to increase sympathy for the Federation, even among those likely to be damaged by its actions. Jamieson in particular began to be much less diffident in expressing his views, and had soon made himself quite unpopular. Before long, indeed, a distinct rift appeared in the Observatory ranks. On the one side were those (mostly the younger men) who felt much as Jamieson did, and regarded Earth as reactionary and intolerant. Against them, on the other hand, were the steady, conservative individuals who would always automatically support those in authority without worrying too much about moral abstractions.

Sadler watched these arguments with great interest, even though he was conscious that the success or failure of his mission had already been decided and that nothing he could do now would alter that. However, there was always the chance that the probably mythical Mr. X might now become careless, or might even attempt to leave the Observatory. Sadler had taken certain steps to guard against this, with the co-operation of the director. No one could get at the spacesuits or tractors without authority, and the base was therefore effectively sealed. Living in a vacuum did have certain advantages from the Security point of view.

The Observatory's state of siege had brought Sadler one tiny triumph, which he could very well have forgone and which seemed an ironic commentary on all his efforts. Jenkins, his suspect from the Stores Section, had been arrested in Central City. When the monorail service had been suspended, he had been in town on very unofficial business, and had been picked up by the agents who had been watching him as a result of Sadler's hunch.

He had been scared of Sadler, and with good reason. But he had never betrayed any state secrets, for he had never possessed any. Like a good many storekeepers before him, he had been busy selling government property.

It was poetic justice. Jenkins' own guilty conscience had caught him. But though Sadler had eliminated one name from his list, the victory gave him very little satisfaction indeed.

The hours dragged on, with tempers getting more and more frayed. Overhead, the sun was now climbing up the morning

95

sky and had now lifted well above the western wall of Plato. The initial sense of emergency had worn off, leaving only a feeling of frustration. One misguided effort was made to organize a concert, but it failed so completely that it left everyone more depressed than before.

Since nothing seemed to be happening, people began to creep up to the surface again, if only to have a look at the sky and to reassure themselves that all was still well. Some of these clandestine excursions caused Sadler much anxiety, but he was able to convince himself that they were quite innocent. Eventually the director recognized the position, by permitting a limited number of people to go up to the observation domes at set hours of the day.

One of the engineers from Power organized a sweepstake, the prizewinner to be the person who guessed how long this peculiar siege was going to last. Everybody in the Observatory contributed, and Sadler—acting on a very long shot—read the lists thoughtfully when they were complete. If there was anyone here who happened to know what the right answer might be, he would take care to avoid winning. That, at least, was the theory. Sadler learned nothing from his study, and finished it wondering just how tortuous his mental processes were becoming. There were times when he feared that he would never be able to think in a straightforward fashion again.

The waiting ended just five days after the Alert. Up on the surface, it was approaching noon, and the Earth had waned to a thin crescent too close to the sun to be looked at with safety. But it was midnight by the Observatory clocks, and Sadler was sleeping when Wagnall unceremoniously entered his room.

"Wake up!" he said, as Sadler rubbed the sleep from his eyes. "The director wants to see you!" Wagnall seemed annoyed at being used as a messenger boy. "There's something going on," he complained, looking at Sadler suspiciously. "He won't even tell *me* what it's all about!"

"I'm not sure that I know either," Sadler replied as he climbed into his dressing gown. He was telling the truth, and on the way to the director's office speculated sleepily on all the things that could possibly have happened.

96

Professor Maclaurin, thought Sadler, had aged a good deal in the last few days. He was no longer the brisk, forceful little man he had been, ruling the Observatory with a rod of iron. There was even a disorderly pile of documents at the side of his once-unsullied desk.

As soon as Wagnall, with obvious reluctance, had left the room, Maclaurin said abruptly:

"What's Carl Steffanson doing on the Moon?"

Sadler blinked uncertainly—he was still not fully awake—and then answered lamely:

"I don't even know who he is. Should I?"

Maclaurin seemed surprised and disappointed.

"I thought your people might have told you he was coming. He's one of the most brilliant physicists we have, in his own specialized field. Central City's just called to say that he's landed—and we've got to get him out to *Mare Imbrium* just as soon as we can, to this place they call Project Thor."

"Why can't he fly there? How do we come into the picture?"

"He was supposed to go by rocket, but the transport's out of action and won't be serviceable for at least six hours. So they're sending him down by monorail, and we're taking him on the last lap by tractor. I've been asked to detail Jamieson for the job. Everyone knows that he's the best tractor driver on the Moon—and he's the only one who's ever been out to Project Thor, whatever *that* is."

"Go on," said Sadler, half suspecting what was coming next.

"I don't trust Jamieson. I don't think it's safe to send him on a mission as important as this one appears to be."

"Is there anyone else who could do it?"

"Not in the time available. It's a very skilled job, and you've no idea how easy it is to lose your way."

"So it has to be Jamieson, it seems. Why do you feel he's a risk?"

"I've listened to him talking in the Common Room. Surely *you've* heard him, too! He's made no secret of his sympathies with the Federation."

Sadler was watching Maclaurin intently while the director was speaking. The indignation—almost the anger—in the little man's voice surprised him. For a moment it raised a fleeting

97

suspicion in his mind: was Maclaurin trying to divert attention from himself?

The vague mistrust lasted only for an instant. There was no need, Sadler realized, to search for deeper motives. Maclaurin was tired and overworked: as Sadler had always suspected, for all his external toughness he was a small man in spirit as well as in stature. He was reacting childishly to his frustration: he had seen his plans disorganized, his whole program brought to a halt—even his precious equipment imperiled. It was all the fault of the Federation, and anyone who did not agree was a potential enemy of Earth.

It was hard not to feel some sympathy for the director; Sadler suspected that he was on the verge of a nervous breakdown, and would have to be handled with extreme care.

"What do you want me to do about it?" he asked in as noncommittal a tone of voice as he could manage.

"I'd like to know if you agree with me about Jamieson. You must have studied him carefully."

"I'm not allowed to discuss my evaluations," Sadler replied. "They're too often based on hearsay and hunches. But I feel that Jamieson's very frankness is a point in his favor. There is a great difference, you know, between dissent and treason."

Maclaurin was silent for a while. Then he shook his head angrily.

"It's too great a risk. I'll not accept the responsibility."

This, thought Sadler, was going to be difficult. He had no authority here, and certainly could not override the director. No one had sent him any instructions; the people who had routed Steffanson through the Observatory probably did not even know that he existed. Liaison between Defense and Central Intelligence was not all that it should be.

But even without instructions, his duty was clear. If Defense wanted to get someone out to Project Thor as urgently as this, they had a very good reason. He must help even if he had to step outside his role of passive observer.

"This is what I suggest, sir," he said briskly. "Interview Jamieson and outline the position to him. Ask him if he'll volunteer for the job. I'll monitor the conversation from the next room and advise you if it's safe to accept. My belief is that if he says he'll do it, he will. Otherwise he'll turn you down flat. I don't think he'll double-cross you."

"You'll go on record over this?"

"Yes," said Sadler, impatiently. "And if I may give some advice, do your best to hide your suspicions. Whatever your own feelings are, be as friendly and open as you can."

Maclaurin thought it over for a while, then shrugged his shoulders in resignation. He flicked the microphone switch.

"Wagnall," he said, "fetch Jamieson here."

To Sadler, waiting in the next room, it seemed hours before anything happened. Then the loudspeaker brought the sound of Jamieson's arrival, and immediately he heard Maclaurin say:

"Sorry to break into your sleep, Jamieson, but we've an urgent job for you. How long would it take you to drive a tractor to Prospect Pass?"

Sadler smiled at the clearly heard gasp of incredulity. He knew exactly what Jamieson was thinking. Prospect was the pass through the southern wall of Plato, overlooking the *Mare Imbrium*. It was avoided by the tractors, which took an easier but more roundabout route a few kilometers to the west. The monocabs, however, went through it without difficulty, and when the lighting was correct gave their passengers one of the most famous views on the Moon—the great sweep down into the *Mare* with the far-off fang of Pico on the skyline.

"If I pushed things, I could do it in an hour. It's only forty kilometers, but very rough going."

"Good," said Maclaurin's voice. "I've just had a message from Central City, asking me to send you out. They know you're our best driver, and you've been there before."

"Been where?" said Jamieson.

"Project Thor. You won't have heard the name, but that's what it's called. The place you drove out to the other night."

"Go on, sir. I'm listening," Jamieson replied. To Sadler, the tension in his voice was obvious.

"This is the position. There's a man in Central City who has to reach Thor immediately. He was supposed to go by rocket, but that's not possible. So they're sending him down here on the monorail, and to save time you'll meet the car out in the pass and take him off. Then you'll drive straight across country to Project Thor. Understand?"

"Not quite. Why can't Thor collect him in one of their own Cats?"

Was Jamieson hedging? wondered Sadler. No, he decided. It was a perfectly reasonable question.

"If you look at the map," said Maclaurin, "you'll see that Prospect is the only convenient place for a tractor to meet the monorail. Moreover, there aren't any really skilled drivers at Thor, it seems. They're sending out a tractor, but you'll probably have finished the job before they can reach Prospect."

There was a long pause. Jamieson was obviously studying the map.

"I'm willing to try it," said Jamieson. "But I'd like to know what it's all about."

Here we go, thought Sadler. I hope Maclaurin does what I told him.

"Very well," Maclaurin replied. "You've a right to know, I suppose. The man who's going to Thor is Dr. Carl Steffanson. And the mission he's engaged on is vital to the security of Earth. That's all I know, but I don't think I need say any more."

Sadler waited, hunched over his speaker, as the long silence dragged on. He knew the decision Jamieson must be making. The young astronomer was discovering that it was one thing to criticize Earth and to condemn her policy when the matter was of no practical importance—and quite another to choose a line of action that might help to bring about her defeat. Sadler had read somewhere that there were plenty of pacifists before the outbreak of war, but few after it had actually started. Jamieson was learning now where his loyalty, if not his logic, lay.

"I'll go," he said at last, so quietly that Sadler could scarcely hear him.

"Remember," insisted Maclaurin, "you have a free choice."

"Have I?" said Jamieson. There was no sarcasm in his voice. He was thinking aloud, talking to himself rather than to the director.

Sadler heard Maclaurin shuffling his papers. "What about your co-driver?" he asked.

"I'll take Wheeler. He went out with me last time."

100

"Very well. You go and fetch him, and I'll get in touch with Transport. And—good luck."

"Thank you, sir."

Sadler waited until he heard the door of Maclaurin's office close behind Jamieson; then he joined the director. Maclaurin looked up at him wearily and said:

"Well?"

"It went off better than I'd feared. I thought you handled it very well."

This was not mere flattery; Sadler was surprised at the way in which Maclaurin had concealed his feelings. Though the interview had not been exactly cordial, there had been no overt unfriendliness.

"I feel much happier," said Maclaurin, "because Wheeler's going with him. He can be trusted."

Despite his worry, Sadler had difficulty in suppressing a smile. He was quite sure that the director's faith in Conrad Wheeler was based largely on that young man's discovery of *Nova Draconis* and his vindication of the Maclaurin Magnitude Integrator. But he needed no further proofs that scientists were just as inclined as anyone else to let their emotions sway their logic.

The desk speaker called for attention.

"The tractor's just leaving, sir. Outer doors opening now."

Maclaurin looked automatically at the wall clock. "That was quick," he said. Then he gazed somberly at Sadler.

"Well, Mr. Sadler, it's too late to do anything about it now. I only hope you're right."

It is seldom realized that driving on the Moon by day is far less pleasant, and even less safe, than driving by night. The merciless glare demands the use of heavy sun filters, and the pools of inky shadow which are always present except on those rare occasions when the sun is vertically overhead can be very dangerous. Often they conceal crevasses which a speeding tractor may be unable to avoid. Driving by Earthlight, on the other hand, involves no such strain. The light is so much softer, the contrasts less extreme.

To make matters worse for Jamieson, he was driving due south—almost directly into the sun. There were times when conditions were so bad that he had to zigzag wildly to avoid the glare from patches of exposed rock ahead. It was not so difficult when they were traveling over dusty regions, but these became fewer and fewer as the ground rose toward the inner ramparts of the mountain wall.

Wheeler knew better than to talk to his friend on this part of the route: Jamieson's task required too much concentration. Presently they were climbing up toward the pass, weaving back and forth along the rugged slopes overlooking the plain. Like fragile tops on the far horizon, the gantries of the great telescopes marked the location of the Observatory. There, thought Wheeler bitterly, was invested millions of man-hours of skill and labor. Now it was doing nothing, and the best that could be hoped was that one day those splendid instruments could once more begin their search into the far places of the universe.

A ridge cut off their view of the plain below, and Jamieson swung round to the right through a narrow valley. Far up the slopes above them, the track of the monorail was now visible, as it came in great, striding leaps down the face of the mountain. There was no way in which a Caterpillar could get up to it, but when they were through the pass they would have no difficulty in driving to within a few meters of the track.

The ground was extremely broken and treacherous here, but drivers who had gone this way before had left markers for the guidance of any who might come after them. Jamieson was using his headlights a good deal now, as he was often working through shadow. On the whole he preferred this to direct sunlight, for he could see the ground ahead much more easily with the steerable beams from the projectors on top of the cab. Wheeler soon took over their operation, and found it fascinating to watch the ovals of light skittering across the rocks. The complete invisibility of the beams themselves, here in the almost perfect vacuum, gave a magical effect to the scene. The light seemed to be coming from nowhere, and to have no connection at all with the tractor.

They reached Prospect fifty minutes after leaving the Observatory, and radioed back their position. From now on, it was only a few kilometers downhill until they came to the rendezvous. The monorail track converged toward their path, then swept on

102

to the south past Pico, a silver thread shrinking out of sight across the face of the Moon.

"Well," said Wheeler with satisfaction, "we haven't kept them waiting. I wish I knew what all this is about."

"Isn't it obvious?" Jamieson answered. "Steffanson's the greatest expert on radiation physics we have. If there's going to be war, surely you realize the sort of weapons that will be used."

"I hadn't thought much about it—it never seemed something to take seriously. Guided missiles, I suppose."

"Very likely, but we should be able to do better than that. Men have been talking about radiation weapons for centuries. If they wanted them, they could make them now."

"Don't say you believe in death-rays!"

"And why not? If you remember your history books, death-rays killed some thousands of people at Hiroshima. And that was a couple of hundred years ago.

"Yes, but it's not difficult to shield against that sort of thing. Can you imagine doing any real *physical* damage with a ray?"

"It would depend on the range. If it was only a few kilometers, I'd say yes. After all, we can generate unlimited amounts of power. By this time we should be able to squirt it all in the same direction if we wanted to. Until today there's been no particular incentive. But now—how do we know what's been going on in secret labs all over the solar system?"

Before Wheeler could reply, he saw the glittering point of light far out across the plain. It was moving toward them with incredible speed, coming up over the horizon like a meteor. Within minutes, it had resolved itself into the blunt-nosed cylinder of the monocab, crouched low over its single track.

"I think I'd better go out and give him a hand," said Jamieson. "He's probably never worn a spacesuit before. He'll certainly have some luggage, too."

Wheeler sat up in the driving position and watched his friend clamber across the rocks to the monorail. The door of the vehicle's emergency airlock opened, and a man stepped out, somewhat unsteadily, onto the Moon. By the way he moved, Wheeler could tell at a glance that he had never been in low gravity before.

Steffanson was carrying a thick briefcase and a large wooden

103

box, which he handled with the utmost care. Jamieson offered to relieve him of these hindrances, but he refused to part with them. His only other baggage was a small traveling-case, which he allowed Jamieson to carry.

The two figures scrambled back down the rocky ramp and Wheeler operated the airlock to let them in. The monocab, having delivered its burden, pulled back into the south and swiftly disappeared the way it had come. It seemed, thought Wheeler, that the driver was in a great hurry to get home. He had never seen one of the cars travel so fast, and for the first time he began to have some faint surmise of the storm that was gathering above this peaceful, sun-drenched landscape. He suspected that they were not the only ones making a rendezvous at Project Thor.

He was right. Far out in space, high above the plane in which Earth and planets swim, the commander of the Federal forces was marshaling his tiny fleet. As a hawk circles above its prey in the moments before its plumeting descent, so Commodore Brennan, lately Professor of Electrical Engineering at the University of Hesperus, held his ships poised above the Moon.

He was waiting for the signal which he still hoped would never come.

Chapter XV

DOCTOR CARL STEFFANSON did not stop to wonder if he was a brave man. Never before in his life had he known the need for so primitive a virtue as physical courage, and he was agreeably surprised at his calmness now that the crisis had almost come. In a few hours, he would probably be dead. The thought gave him more annoyance than fear; there was so much work he wanted to do, so many theories to be tested. It would be wonderful to get back to scientific research again, after the rat-race of the last two years. But that was day-dreaming; mere survival was as much as he could hope for now.

He opened his briefcase and pulled out the sheafs of wiring diagrams and component schedules. With some amusement, he noticed that Wheeler was staring with frank curiosity at the complex circuits and the SECRET labels plastered over them. Well, there was little need for security now, and Steffanson himself could not have made much sense of these circuits had he not invented them himself.

He glanced again at the packing case to make sure that it was securely lashed down. There, in all probability, lay the future of more worlds than one. How many other men had ever been sent on a mission like this? Steffanson could think of but two examples, both back in the days of the Second World War. There had been a British scientist who had carried a small box across the Atlantic, containing what was later called the most valuable consignment ever to reach the shores of the United States. That had been the first cavity magnetron, the invention which made radar the key weapon of war and destroyed the power of Hitler. Then, a few years later, there had been a plane flying across the Pacific to the island of Tinian, carrying almost all the free uranium 235 then in existence. . . .

But neither of those missions, for all their importance, had the urgency of this.

Steffanson had exchanged only a few words of formal greeting with Jamieson and Wheeler, expressing his thanks at their cooperation. He knew nothing about them, except that they were astronomers from the Observatory who had volunteered to undertake this trip. Since they were scientists, they would certainly be curious to know what he was doing here, and he was not surprised when Jamieson handed over the controls to his colleague and stepped down from the driving position.

"It won't be so rough from now on," said Jamieson. "We'll get to this Thor place in about twenty minutes. Is that good enough for you?"

Steffanson nodded.

"That's better than we'd hoped, when that damn ship broke down. You'll probably get a special medal for this."

"I'm not interested," said Jamieson rather coldly. "All I want to do is what's right. Are you quite certain that you're doing the same?"

Steffanson looked at him in surprise, but it took him only an instant to sum up the situation. He had met Jamieson's type before among the younger men of his own staff. These idealists all went through the same mental heart-searchings. And they would all grow out of it when they were older. He sometimes wondered if that was a tragedy or a blessing.

"You are asking me," he said quietly, "to predict the future. No man can ever tell if, in the long run, his acts will lead to good or evil. But I am working for the defense of Earth, and if there is an attack it will come from the Federation, not from us. I think you should bear that in mind."

"Yet haven't we provoked it?"

"Perhaps so, but again there is much to be said on both sides. You think of the Federals as starry-eyed pioneers, building wonderful new civilizations out there on the planets. You forget that they can be tough and unscrupulous, too. If they get what they want, they'll be intolerable. I'm afraid they've asked for a lesson, and we hope to give it to them. It's a pity it's come to this, but I see no alternative."

He glanced at his watch, saw that it was nearly at the hour, and continued: "Do you mind switching on the news? I'd like to hear the latest developments."

Jamieson tuned in the set, and rotated the antenna system toward Earth. There was a fair amount of noise from the solar background, for Earth was now almost in line with the sun, but the sheer power of the station made the message perfectly intelligible and there was no trace of fading.

Steffanson was surprised to see that the tractor chronograph was over a second fast. Then he realized that it was set for that oddly christened hybrid, Lunar Greenwich Time. The signal he was listening to had just bridged the four-hundred-thousand-kilometer gulf from Earth. It was a chilling reminder of his remoteness from home.

Then there was a delay so long that Jamieson turned up the volume to check that the set was still operating. After a full minute, the announcer spoke, his voice striving desperately to be as impersonal as ever.

"This is Earth calling. The following statement has been issued from the Hague:

"The Triplanetary Federation has informed the government of Earth that it intends to seize certain portions of the Moon, and that any attempt to resist this action will be countered by force.

"This government is taking all necessary steps to preserve the integrity of the Moon. A further announcement will be issued as soon as possible. For the present it is emphasized that there is no immediate danger, as there are no hostile ships within twenty hours of Earth.

"This is Earth. Stand by."

A sudden silence fell; only the hiss of the carrier-wave and the occasional crackle of solar static still issued from the speaker. Wheeler had brought the tractor to a halt so that he could hear the announcement. From his driving seat, he looked down at the little tableau in the cabin beneath him. Steffanson was staring at the circuit diagrams spread over the map table, but was obviously not seeing them. Jamieson still stood with his hand on the volume control; he had not moved since the beginning of the announcement. Then, without a word, he climbed up into the driving cab, and took over from Wheeler.

To Steffanson, it seemed ages before Wheeler called to him: "We're nearly there! Look—dead ahead." He went to the forward observation port, and stared across the cracked and broken ground. What a place to fight for, he thought. But, of course, this barren wilderness of lava and meteor dust was only a disguise. Beneath it Nature had hidden treasures which men had taken two hundred years to find. Perhaps it would have been better had they never found them at all. . . .

Still two or three kilometers ahead, the great metal dome was glinting in the sunlight. From this angle, it had an astonishing appearance, for the segment in shadow was so dark as to be almost invisible. At first sight, indeed, it looked as if the dome had been bisected by some enormous knife. The whole place looked utterly deserted, but within, Steffanson knew, it would be a hive of furious activity. He prayed that his assistants had completed the wiring of the power and sub-modulator circuits.

Steffanson began to adjust the helmet of his spacesuit, which he had not bothered to take off after entering the tractor. He stood behind Jamieson, holding on to one of the storage racks to steady himself.

"Now that we're here," he said, "the least I can do is to let

107

you understand what's happened." He gestured toward the rapidly approaching dome. "This place started as a mine, and it still is. We've achieved something that's never been done before—drilled a hole a hundred kilometers deep, right through the Moon's crust and down into really rich deposits of metal."

"A hundred kilometers!" cried Wheeler. "That's impossible! No hole could stay open under the pressure."

"It can and does," retorted Steffanson. "I've not time to discuss the technique, even if I knew much about it. But remember you can drill a hole six times as deep on the Moon as you can on Earth, before it caves in. However, that's only part of the story. The real secret lies in what they've called pressure-mining. As fast as it's sunk, the well is filled with a heavy silicone oil, the same density as the rocks around it. So no matter how far down you go, the pressure is the same inside as out, and there's no tendency for the hole to close. Like most simple ideas, it's taken a lot of skill to put it into practice. All the operating equipment has to work submerged, under enormous pressure, but the problems are being overcome and we believe we can get metals out in worthwhile quantities.

"The Federation learned this was going on about two years ago. We believe they've tried the same thing, but without any luck. So they're determined that if they can't share this hoard, we won't have it either. Their policy seems to be one of bullying us into co-operation, and it's not going to work.

"That's the background, but now it's only the less important part of the story. There are weapons here as well. Some have been completed and tested, others are waiting for the final adjustments. I'm bringing the key components for what may be the decisive one. That's why Earth may owe you a greater debt than it can ever pay. Don't interrupt—we're nearly there and this is what I really want to tell you. The radio was not telling the truth about that twenty hours of safety. That's what the Federation wants us to believe, and we hope they go on thinking we've been fooled. But we've spotted their ships, and they're approaching ten times as fast as anything that's ever moved through space before. I'm afraid they've got a fundamental new method of propulsion—I only hope it hasn't given them new weapons as well. We've not much more than three hours before they get here, assuming they don't step up their speed still further. You could stay, but for your own safety I advise you to turn around and drive like hell back to the Observatory. If anything starts to happen while you're still out in the open, get under cover as quickly as possible. Go down into a crevasse—anywhere you can find shelter—and stay there until it's all over. Now good-by and good luck. I hope we have a chance of meeting again, when this business is finished."

Still clutching his mysterious packing case, Steffanson disappeared into the airlock before either of the men could speak. They were now entering the shadows of the great dome, and Jamieson circled it looking for an opening. Presently he recognized the spot through which he and Wheeler had made their entrance, and brought Ferdinand to a halt.

The outer door of the tractor slammed shut and the "Airlock Clear" indicator flashed on. They saw Steffanson running across toward the dome, and with perfect timing a circular port flipped open to let him in, then snapped shut behind him.

The tractor was alone in the building's enormous shadow. Nowhere else was there any sign of life, but suddenly the metal framework of the machine began to vibrate at a steadily rising frequency. The meters on the control panel wavered madly, the lights dimmed, and then it was all over. Everything was normal again, but some tremendous field of force had swept out from the dome and was even now expanding into space. It left the two men with an overwhelming impression of energies awaiting the signal for their release. They began to understand the urgency of Steffanson's warning. The whole deserted landscape seemed tense with expectation.

Across the steeply curving plain, the tiny beetle of the tractor raced for the safety of the distant hills. But could they be sure of safety even there? Jamieson doubted it. He remembered the weapons that science had made more than two centuries ago; they would be merely the foundation upon which the arts of war could build today. The silent land around him, now burning beneath the noonday sun, might soon be blasted by radiations fiercer still.

He drove forward into the shadow of the tractor, toward the

109

ramparts of Plato, towering along the skyline like some fortress of the giants. But the real fortress was behind him, preparing its unknown weapons for the ordeal that must come.

Chapter XVI

IT WOULD NEVER HAVE HAPPENED had Jamieson been thinking more of driving and less of politics—though, in the circumstances, he could hardly be blamed. The ground ahead looked level and firm—exactly the same as the kilometers they had already safely traversed.

It was level, but it was no firmer than water. Jamieson knew what had happened the moment that Ferdinand's engine started to race, and the tractor's nose disappeared in a great cloud of dust. The whole vehicle tilted forward, began to rock madly to and fro, and then lost speed despite all that Jamieson could do. Like a ship foundering in a heavy sea, it started to sink. To Wheeler's horrified eyes, they seemed to be going under in swirling clouds of spray. Within seconds, the sunlight around them had vanished. Jamieson had stopped the motor; in a silence broken only by the murmur of the air circulators, they were sinking below the surface of the Moon.

The cabin lights came on as Jamieson found the switch. For a moment, both men were too stunned to do anything but sit and stare helplessly at each other. Then Wheeler walked, not very steadily, to the nearest observation window. He could see absolutely nothing: no night was ever as dark as this. A smooth velvet curtain might have been brushing the other side of the thick quartz, for all the light that could penetrate it.

Suddenly, with a gentle but distinct bump, Ferdinand reached the bottom.

"Thank God for that," breathed Jamieson. "It's not very deep."

"What good does that do us?" asked Wheeler, hardly daring to believe there was any hope. He had heard too many horrifying tales of these treacherous dust bowls, and the men and tractors they had engulfed.

The lunar dust bowls are, fortunately, less common than might be imagined from some travelers' tales, for they can occur only under rather special conditions, which even now are not fully understood. To make one, it is necessary to start with a shallow crater pit in the right kind of rock, and then wait a few hundred million years while the temperature changes between night and day slowly pulverize the surface layers. As this age-long process continues, so a finer and finer grade of dust is produced, until at last it begins to flow like a liquid and accumulates at the bottom of the crater. In almost all respects, indeed, it *is* a liquid: it is so incredibly fine that if collected in a bucket, it will slop around like a rather mobile oil. At night one can watch convection currents circulating in it, as the upper layers cool and descend, and the warmer dust at the bottom rises to the top. This effect makes dust bowls easy to locate, since infra-red detectors can "see" their abnormal heat radiation at distances of several kilometers. However, during the daytime this method is useless owing to the masking effect of the sun.

"There's no need to get alarmed," said Jamieson, though he looked none too happy. "I think we can get out of this. It must be a very small bowl, or it would have been spotted before. This area's supposed to have been thoroughly marked."

"It's big enough to have swallowed us."

"Yes, but don't forget what this stuff's like. As long as we can keep the motors running, we have a chance of pushing our way out—like a submarine-tank making its way up on to shore. The thing that bothers me is whether we should go ahead, or try and back out."

"If we go ahead, we might get in deeper."

"Not necessarily. As I said, it must be a pretty small bowl and our momentum may have carried us more than halfway across it. Which way would you say the floor is tilted now?"

"The front seems to be a bit higher than the rear."

"That's what I thought. I'm going ahead—we can get more power that way, too."

Very gently, Jamieson engaged the clutch in the lowest possible gear. The tractor shook and protested, then lurched forward a few centimeters, then halted again.

"I was afraid of that," said Jamieson. "I can't keep up a steady

111

progress. We'll have to go in jerks. Pray for the engine—not to mention the transmission."

They jolted their way forward in agonizingly slow surges, then Jamieson cut the engine completely.

"Why did you do that?" Wheeler asked anxiously. "We seemed to be getting somewhere."

"Yes, but we're also getting too hot. This dust is an almost perfect heat insulator. We'll have to wait a minute until we cool off."

Neither felt like making any conversation as they sat in the brightly lit cabin that might well, Wheeler reflected, become their tomb. It was ironic that they had encountered this mishap while they were racing for safety.

"Do you hear that noise?" said Jamieson suddenly. He switched off the air-circulator, so that complete silence fell inside the cab.

There was the faintest of sounds coming through the walls. It was a sort of whispering rustle, and Wheeler could not imagine what it was.

"The dust's starting to rise. It's highly unstable, you know, and even a small amount of heat is enough to start convection currents. I expect we're making quite a little geyser up at the top—it will help anyone to find us if they come and look."

That was some consolation, at any rate. They had air and food for many days—all tractors carried a large emergency reserve—and the Observatory knew their approximate position. But before long the Observatory might have trouble of its own, and would be unable to bother about them. . . .

Jamieson re-started the motor, and the sturdy vehicle started to butt its way forward again through the dry quicksand that enveloped them. It was impossible to tell how much progress they were making, and Wheeler dared not imagine what would happen if the motors failed. The caterpillar treads were grinding at the rock beneath them, and the whole tractor shook and groaned under the intolerable load.

It was almost an hour before they were certain they were getting somewhere. The floor of the tractor was definitely tilting upward, but there was no way of telling how far below the quasi-liquid surface they were still submerged. They might emerge at

112

any moment into the blessed light of day—or they might have a hundred meters still to traverse at this snail-like pace.

Jamieson was stopping for longer and longer intervals, which might reduce the strain on the engine but did nothing to reduce that on the passengers. During one of these pauses Wheeler asked him outright what they should do if they could get no further.

"We've only two possibilities," Jamieson answered. "We can stay here and hope to be rescued—which won't be as bad as it sounds, since our tracks will make it obvious where we are. The other alternative is to go out."

"What! That's impossible!"

"Not at all. I know a case where it's been done. It would be rather like escaping from a sunken submarine."

"It's a horrible thought—trying to swim through this stuff."

"I was once caught in a snowdrift when I was a kid, so I can guess what it would be like. The great danger would be losing your direction and floundering around in circles until you were exhausted. Let's hope we don't have to try the experiment."

It was a long time, Wheeler decided, since he had heard a bigger understatement than that.

The driving cab emerged above the dust level about an hour later, and no men could ever have greeted the sun with such joy. But they had not yet reached safety; though Ferdinand could make better speed as the resistance slackened, there might still be unsuspected depths ahead of them.

Wheeler watched with fascinated repulsion as the horrible stuff eddied past the tractor. At times it was quite impossible to believe that they were not forcing their way through a liquid, and only the slowness with which they moved spoiled the illusion. He wondered if it was worth suggesting that in future Caterpillars have better streamlining to improve their chances in emergencies like this. Who would ever have dreamed, back on Earth, that *that* sort of thing might be necessary?

At last Ferdinand crawled up to the security of the dry land, which, after all, was no drier than the deadly lake from which they had escaped. Jamieson, almost exhausted by the strain, slumped down across the control panel. The reaction had left

Wheeler shaken and weak, but he was too thankful to be out of danger to let that worry him.

He had forgotten, in the relief of seeing sunlight again, that they had left Project Thor three hours ago, and had covered less than twenty kilometers.

Even so, they might have made it. But they had just started on their way again, and were crawling over the top of a quite gentle ridge, when there was a scream of tearing metal and Ferdinand tried to spin round in a circle. Jamieson cut the motor instantly and they came to rest broadside-on to their direction of motion.

"And that," said Jamieson softly, "is most definitely that. But I don't think we're in a position to grumble. If the starboard transmission had sheared while we were still in that dust bowl——" He didn't finish the sentence, but turned to the observation port that looked back along their trail. Wheeler followed his gaze.

The dome of Project Thor was still visible on the horizon. Perhaps they had already strained their luck to the utmost, but it would have been nice could they have put the protecting curve of the Moon clear between themselves and the unknown storms that were brewing there.

Chapter XVII

EVEN TODAY, little has ever been revealed concerning the weapons used in the Battle of Pico. It is known that missiles played only a minor part in the engagement. In space warfare, anything short of a direct hit is almost useless, since there is nothing to transmit the energy of a shock wave. An atom bomb exploding a few hundred meters away can cause no blast damage, and even its radiation can do little harm to well-protected structures. Moreover, both Earth and the Federation had effective means of diverting ordinary projectiles.

Purely non-material weapons would have to play the greatest role. The simplest of these were the ion-beams, developed directly from the drive-units of spaceships. Since the invention of the first radio tubes, almost three centuries before, men had been learning how to produce and focus ever more concentrated streams of charged particles. The climax had been reached in spaceship propulsion with the so-called "ion rocket," generating its thrust from the emission of intense beams of electrically charged particles. The deadliness of these beams had caused many accidents in space, even though they were deliberately defocused to limit their effective range.

There was, of course, an obvious answer to such weapons. The electric and magnetic fields which produced them could also be used for their dispersion, converting them from annihilating beams into a harmless, scattered spray.

More effective, but more difficult to build, were the weapons using pure radiation. Yet even here, both Earth and the Federation had succeeded. It remained to be seen which had done the better job—the superior science of the Federation, or the greater productive capacity of Earth.

Commodore Brennan was well aware of all these factors as his little fleet converged upon the Moon. Like all commanders, he was going into action with fewer resources than he would have wished. Indeed, he would very much have preferred not to be going into action at all.

The converted liner *Eridanus* and the largely rebuilt freighter *Lethe*—once listed in Lloyd's register as the *Morning Star* and the *Rigel*—would now be swinging in between Earth and Moon along their carefully plotted courses. He did not know if they still had the element of surprise. Even if they had been detected, Earth might not know of the existence of this third and largest ship, the *Acheron*. Brennan wondered what romantic with a taste for mythology was responsible for these names—probably Commissioner Churchill, who made a point of emulating his famous ancestor in as many ways as he possibly could. Yet they were not inappropriate. The rivers of Death and Oblivion—yes, these were things they might bring to many men before another day had passed.

Lieutenant Curtis, one of the few men in the crew who had actually spent most of his working life in space, looked up from the communications desk.

"Message just picked up from the Moon, sir. Addressed to us."

Brennan was badly shaken. If they had been spotted, surely their opponents were not so contemptuous of them that they would freely admit the fact! He glanced quickly at the signal, then gave a sigh of relief.

OBSERVATORY TO FEDERATION. WISH TO REMIND YOU OF EXISTENCE IRREPLACEABLE INSTRUMENTS PLATO. ALSO ENTIRE OBSERVATORY STAFF STILL HERE. MACLAURIN. DIRECTOR.

"Don't frighten me like that again, Curtis," said the commodore. "I thought you meant it was beamed at me. I'd hate to think they could detect us this far out."

"Sorry, sir. It's just a general broadcast. They're still sending it out on the Observatory wavelength."

Brennan handed the signal over to his operations controller, Captain Merton.

"What do you make of this? You worked there, didn't you?"

Merton smiled as he read the message.

"Just like Maclaurin. Instruments first, staff second. I'm not too worried. I'll do my damnedest to miss him. A hundred kilometers isn't a bad safety margin, when you come to think of it. Unless there's a direct hit with a stray, they've nothing to worry about. They're pretty well dug in, you know."

The relentless hand of the chronometer was scything away the last minutes. Still confident that his ship, encased in its cocoon of night, had not yet been detected, Commodore Brennan watched the three sparks of his fleet creep along their appointed tracks in the plotting sphere. This was not a destiny he had ever imagined would be his—to hold the fate of worlds within his hands.

But he was not thinking of the powers that slumbered in the reactor banks, waiting for his command. He was not concerned with the place he would take in history, when men looked back upon this day. He only wondered, as had all who had ever faced battle for the first time, where he would be this same time tomorrow.

Less than a million kilometers away, Carl Steffanson sat at a control desk and watched the image of the sun, picked up by one of the many cameras that were the eyes of Project Thor. The group of tired technicians standing around him had almost completed the equipment before his arrival; now the discriminating units he had brought from Earth in such desperate haste had been wired into the circuit.

Steffanson turned a knob, and the sun went out. He flicked from one camera position to another, but all the eyes of the fortress were equally blind. The coverage was complete.

Too weary to feel any exhilaration, he leaned back in his seat and gestured toward the controls.

"It's up to you now. Set it to pass enough light for vision, but to give total rejection from the ultra-violet upward. We're sure none of their beams carry any effective power much beyond a thousand Angstroms. They'll be very surprised when all their stuff bounces off. I only wish we could send it back the way it came."

"Wonder what we look like from outside when the screen's on?" said one of the engineers.

"Just like a perfectly reflecting mirror. As long as it keeps reflecting, we're safe against pure radiation. That's all I can promise you."

Steffanson looked at his watch.

"If Intelligence is correct, we have about twenty minutes to spare. But I shouldn't count on it."

"At least Maclaurin knows where we are now," said Jamieson as he switched off the radio. "But I can't blame him for not sending someone to pull us out."

"Then what do we do now?"

"Get some food," Jamieson answered, walking back to the tiny galley. "I think we've earned it, and there may be a long walk ahead of us."

Wheeler looked nervously across the plain, to the distant but all too clearly visible dome of Project Thor. Then his jaw dropped and it was some seconds before he could believe that his eyes were not playing tricks on him.

"Sid!" he called. "Come and look at this!"

117

Jamieson joined him at a rush, and together they stared out toward the horizon. The partly shadowed hemisphere of the dome had changed its appearance completely. Instead of a thin crescent of light, it now showed a single dazzling star, as though the image of the sun was being reflected from a perfectly spherical mirror surface.

The telescope confirmed this impression. The dome itself was no longer visible; its place seemed to have been taken by this fantastic silver apparition. To Wheeler it looked exactly like a great blob of mercury sitting on the skyline.

"I'd like to know how they've done that," was Jamieson's unexcited comment. "Some kind of interference effect, I suppose. It must be part of their defense system."

"We'd better get moving," said Wheeler anxiously. "I don't like the look of this. It feels horribly exposed up here."

Jamieson had started throwing open cupboards and pulling out stores. He tossed some bars of chocolate and packets of compressed meat over to Wheeler.

"Start chewing some of this," he said. "We won't have time for a proper meal now. Better have a drink as well, if you're thirsty. But don't take too much—you'll be in that suit for hours, and these aren't luxury models."

Wheeler was doing some mental arithmetic. They must be about eighty kilometers from base, with the entire rampart of Plato between them and the Observatory. Yes, it would be a long walk home, and they might after all be safer here. The tractor, which had already served them so well, could protect them from a good deal of trouble.

Jamieson toyed with the idea, but then rejected it. "Remember what Steffanson said," he reminded Wheeler. "He told us to get underground as soon as we could. And he must know what he's talking about."

They found a crevasse within fifty meters of the tractor, on the slope of the ridge away from the fortress. It was just deep enough to see out of when they stood upright, and the floor was sufficiently level to lie down. As a slit trench, it might almost have been made to order, and Jamieson felt much happier when he had located it.

"The only thing that worries me now," he said, "is how long

we may have to wait. It's still possible that nothing will happen at all. On the other hand, if we start walking we may be caught in the open away from shelter."

After some discussion, they decided on a compromise. They would keep their suits on, but would go back and sit in Ferdinand where at least they would be comfortable. It would take them only a few seconds to get to the trench.

There was no warning of any kind. Suddenly the gray, dusty rocks of the Sea of Rains were scorched by a light they had never known before in all their history. Wheeler's first impression was that someone had turned a giant searchlight full upon the tractor; then he realized that this sun-eclipsing explosion was many kilometers away. High above the horizon was a ball of violet flame, perfectly spherical, and rapidly losing brilliance as it expanded. Within seconds, it had faded to a great cloud of luminous gas. It was dropping down toward the edge of the Moon, and almost at once had sunk below the skyline like some fantastic sun.

"We were fools," said Jamieson gravely. "That was an atomic warhead—we may be dead men already."

"Nonsense," retorted Wheeler, though without much confidence. "That was fifty kilometers away. The gammas would be pretty weak by the time they reached us—and these walls aren't bad shielding."

Jamieson did not answer; he was already on his way to the airlock. Wheeler started to follow him, then remembered that there was a radiation detector aboard and went back to collect it. Was there anything else that might be useful while he was here? On a sudden impulse, he jerked down the curtain-rod above the little alcove that concealed the lavatory, then ripped away the wall mirror over the sink.

When he joined Jamieson, who was waiting impatiently for him in the airlock, he handed over the detector, but did not bother to explain the rest of his equipment. Not until they had settled down in their trench, which they reached without further incident, did he make its purpose clear.

"If there's one thing I hate," he said petulantly, "it's not being able to see what's going on." He started to fix the mirror to the curtain rod, using some wire from one of the pouches round his suit. After a couple of minutes' work, he was able to hoist a crude periscope out of the hole.

"I can just see the dome," he said, with some satisfaction. "It's quite unchanged, as far as I can tell."

"It would be," Jamieson replied. "They must have managed to explode that bomb somehow while it was miles away."

"Perhaps it was only a warning shot."

"Not likely! No one wastes plutonium for firework displays. That meant business. I wonder when the next move is going to be?"

It did not come for another five minutes. Then, almost simultaneously, three more of the dazzling atomic suns burst against the sky. They were all moving on trajectories that took them toward the dome, but long before they reached it they had dispersed into tenuous clouds of vapor.

"Rounds one and two to Earth," muttered Wheeler. "I wonder where these missiles are coming from?"

"If any of them burst directly overhead," said Jamieson, "we *will* be done for. Don't forget that there's no atmosphere to absorb the gammas here."

"What does the radiation meter say?"

"Nothing much yet, but I'm worried about that first blast, when we were still in the tractor."

Wheeler was too busily searching the sky to answer. Somewhere up there among the stars, which he could see now that he was out of the direct glare of the sun, must be the ships of the Federation, preparing for the next attack. It was not likely that the ships themselves would be visible, but he might be able to see their weapons in action.

From somewhere beyond Pico, six sheaves of flame shot up into the sky at an enormous acceleration. The dome was launching its first missiles, straight into the face of the sun. The *Lethe* and the *Eridanus* were using a trick as old as warfare itself; they were approaching from a direction in which their opponent would be partly blinded. Even radar could be distracted by the background of solar interference, and Commodore Brennan had enlisted two large sunspots as minor allies.

Within seconds, the rockets were lost in the glare. Minutes seemed to pass; then the sunlight abruptly multiplied itself a hundredfold. The folks up on Earth, thought Wheeler as he readjusted the filters of his visor, will be having a grandstand view tonight. And the atmosphere which is such a nuisance to astronomers will protect them from anything that these warheads can radiate.

There was no way to tell if the missiles had done any damage. That enormous and soundless explosion might have dissipated itself harmlessly into space. This would be a strange battle, he realized. He might never even see the Federation ships, which would almost certainly be painted as black as night to make them undetectable.

Then he saw that something was happening to the dome. It was no longer a gleaming spherical mirror reflecting only the single image of the sun. Light was splashing from it in all directions, and its brilliance was increasing second by second. From somewhere out in space, power was being poured into the fortress. That could only mean that the ships of the Federation were floating up there against the stars, beaming countless millions of kilowatts down upon the Moon. But there was still no sign of them, for there was nothing to reveal the track of the river of energy pouring invisibly through space.

The dome was now far too bright to look upon directly, and Wheeler readjusted his filters. He wondered when it was going to reply to the attack, or indeed if it could do so while it was under this bombardment. Then he saw that the hemisphere was surrounded by a wavering corona, like some kind of brush discharge. Almost at the same moment, Jamieson's voice rang in his ears.

"Look, Con—right overhead!"

He glanced away from the mirror and looked directly into the sky. For the first time, he saw one of the Federation ships. Though he did not know it, he was seeing the *Acheron*, the only spaceship ever to be built specifically for war. It was clearly visible, and seemed remarkably close. Between it and the fortress, like an impalpable shield, flared a disk of light which as he watched turned cherry-red, then blue-white, then the deadly searing violet seen only in the hottest of the stars. The shield wavered back and forth, giving the impression of being balanced by tremendous and opposing energies. As Wheeler stared, oblivious to his peril, he saw that the whole ship was surrounded by a faint halo of light, brought to incandescence only where the weapons of the fortress tore against it.

It was some time before he realized that there were two other ships in the sky, each shielded by its own flaming nimbus. Now the battle was beginning to take shape; each side had cautiously tested its defenses and its weapons, and only now had the real trial of strength begun.

The two astronomers stared in wonder at the moving fireballs of the ships. Here was something totally new—something far more important than any mere weapon. These vessels possessed a means of propulsion which must make the rocket obsolete. They could hover motionless at will, then move off in any direction at a high acceleration. They needed this mobility; the fortress, with all its fixed equipment, far outpowered them and much of their defense lay in their speed.

In utter silence, the battle was rising to its climax. Millions of years ago the molten rock had frozen to form the Sea of Rains, and now the weapons of the ships were turning it once more to lava. Out by the fortress, clouds of incandescent vapor were being blasted into the sky as the beams of the attackers spent their fury against the unprotected rocks. It was impossible to tell which side was inflicting the greater damage. Now and again a screen would flare up, as a flicker of heat passes over white-hot steel. When that happened to one of the battleships, it would move away with that incredible acceleration, and it would be several seconds before the focusing devices of the fort had located it again.

Both Wheeler and Jamieson were surprised that the battle was being fought at such short ranges. There was probably never more than a hundred kilometers between the antagonists, and usually it was much less than this. When one fought with weapons that traveled at the speed of light—indeed, when one fought with light itself—such distances were trivial.

The explanation did not occur to them until the end of the engagement. All radiation weapons have one limitation: they must obey the law of inverse squares. Only explosive missiles are equally effective from whatever range they have been projected: if one is hit by an atomic bomb, it makes no difference whether it has traveled ten kilometers or a thousand.

But double the distance of any kind of radiation weapon, and you divide its power by four owing to the spreading of the beam. No wonder, therefore, that the Federal commander was coming as close to his objective as he dared.

The fort, lacking mobility, had to accept any punishment the ships could give it. After the battle had been on for a few minutes, it was impossible for the unshielded eye to look anywhere toward the south. Ever and again the clouds of rock vapor would go sailing up into the sky, falling back on the ground like luminous steam. And presently, as he peered through his darkened goggles and maneuvered his clumsy periscope, Wheeler saw something he could scarcely believe. Around the base of the fortress was a slowly spreading circle of lava, melting down ridges and even small hillocks like lumps of wax.

That awe-inspiring sight brought home to him, as nothing else had done, the frightful power of the weapons that were being wielded only a few kilometers away. If even the merest stray reflection of those energies reached them here, they would be snuffed out of existence as swiftly as moths in an oxy-hydrogen flame.

The three ships appeared to be moving in some complex tactical pattern, so that they could maintain the maximum bombardment of the fort while reducing its opportunity of striking back. Several times one of the ships passed vertically overhead, and Wheeler retreated as far into the crack as he could in case any of the radiation scattered from the screens splashed down upon them. Jamieson, who had given up trying to persuade his colleague to take fewer risks, had now crawled some distance along the crevasse, looking for a deeper part, preferably with a good overhang. He was not so far away, however, that the rock was shielding the suit-radios, and Wheeler gave him a continuous commentary on the battle.

It was hard to believe that the entire engagement had not yet lasted ten minutes. As Wheeler cautiously surveyed the inferno to the south, he noticed that the hemisphere seemed to have lost some of its symmetry. At first he thought that one of the generators might have failed, so that the protective field could no longer be maintained. Then he saw that the lake of lava was at least a kilometer across, and he guessed that the whole fort had floated off its foundations. Probably the defenders were not even aware of the fact. Their insulation must be taking care of solar heats, and would hardly notice the modest warmth of molten rock.

And now a strange thing was beginning to happen. The rays with which the battle was being fought were no longer quite invisible, for the fortress was no longer in a vacuum. Around it the boiling rock was releasing enormous volumes of gas, through which the paths of the rays were as clearly visible as searchlights in a misty night on Earth. At the same time Wheeler began to notice a continual hail of tiny particles around him. For a moment he was puzzled; then he realized that the rock vapor was condensing after it had been blasted up into the sky. It seemed too light to be dangerous, and he did not mention it to Jamieson—it would only give him something else to worry about. As long as the dust fall was not too heavy, the normal insulation of the suits could deal with it. In any case, it would probably be quite cold by the time it got back to the surface.

The tenuous and temporary atmosphere round the dome was producing another unexpected effect. Occasional flashes of lightning darted between ground and sky, draining off the enormous static charges that must be accumulating around the fort. Some of those flashes would have been spectacular by themselves—but they were scarcely visible against the incandescent clouds that generated them.

Accustomed though he was to the eternal silences of the Moon, Wheeler still felt a sense of unreality at the sight of these tremendous forces striving together without the least whisper of sound. Sometimes a gentle vibration would reach him, perhaps the rock-borne concussion of falling lava. But much of the time, he had the feeling that he was watching a television program when the sound had failed.

Afterward, he could hardly believe he had been such a fool as to expose himself to the risks he was running now. At the moment, he felt no fear—only an immense curiosity and excitement. He had been caught, though he did not know it, by the deadly glamor of war. There is a fatal strain in men that, whatever reason may say, makes their hearts beat faster when they watch the colors flying and hear the ancient music of the drums.

Curiously enough, Wheeler did not feel any sense of identification with either side. It seemed to him, in his present abnormally overwrought mood, that all this was a vast, impersonal display arranged for his special benefit. He felt something approaching contempt for Jamieson, who was missing everything by seeking safety.

Perhaps the real truth of the matter was that having just escaped from one peril, Wheeler was in the exalted state, akin to drunkenness, in which the idea of personal danger seems absurd. He had managed to get out of the dust bowl—nothing else could harm him now.

Jamieson had no such consolation. He saw little of the battle, but felt its terror and grandeur far more deeply than his friend. It was too late for regrets, but over and over again he wrestled with his conscience. He felt angry at fate for having placed him in such a position that his action might have decided the destiny of worlds. He was angry, in equal measure, with Earth and the Federation for having let matters come to this. And he was sick at heart as he thought of the future toward which the human race might now be heading.

Wheeler never knew why the fortress waited so long before it used its main weapon. Perhaps Steffanson—or whoever was in charge—was waiting for the attack to slacken so that he could risk lowering the defenses of the dome for the millisecond that he needed to launch his stiletto.

Wheeler saw it strike upward, a solid bar of light stabbing at the stars. He remembered the rumors that had gone round the Observatory. So *this* was what had been seen, flashing above the mountains. He did not have time to reflect on the staggering violation of the laws of optics which this phenomenon implied, for he was staring at the ruined ship above his head. The beam had gone through the *Lethe* as if she did not exist; the fortress had speared her as an entomologist pierces a butterfly with a pin.

Whatever one's loyalties, it was a terrible thing to see how the screens of that great ship suddenly vanished as her generators died, leaving her helpless and unprotected in the sky. The secondary weapons of the fort were at her instantly, tearing out great gashes of metal and boiling away her armor layer by layer. Then, quite slowly, she began to settle toward the Moon, still on an even keel. No one will ever know what stopped her, probably some short-circuit in her controls, since none of her crew could have been left alive. For suddenly she went off to the east in a long, flat trajectory. By that time most of her hull had been boiled away and the skeleton of her framework was almost completely exposed. The crash came, minutes later, as she plunged out of sight beyond the Teneriffe Mountains. A blue-white aurora flickered for a moment below the horizon, and Wheeler waited for the shock to reach him.

And then, as he stared into the east, he saw a line of dust rising from the plain, sweeping toward him as if driven by a mighty wind. The concussion was racing through the rock, hurling the surface dust high into the sky as it passed. The swift, inexorable approach of that silently moving wall, advancing at the rate of several kilometers a second, was enough to strike terror into anyone who did not know its cause. But it was quite harmless; when the wave-front reached him, it was as if a minor earthquake had passed. The veil of dust reduced visibility to zero for a few seconds, then subsided as swiftly as it had come.

When Wheeler looked again for the remaining ships, they were so far away that their screens had shrunk to little balls of fire against the zenith. At first he thought they were retreating; then, abruptly, the screens began to expand as they came down into the attack under a terrific vertical acceleration. Over by the fortress the lava, like some tortured living creature, was throwing itself madly into the sky as the beams tore into it.

The *Acheron* and *Eridanus* came out of their dives about a kilometer above the fort. For an instant, they were motionless; then they went back into the sky together. But the *Eridanus* had been mortally wounded, though Wheeler knew only that one of the screens was shrinking much more slowly than the other. With a feeling of helpless fascination, he watched the stricken ship fall back toward the Moon. He wondered if the fort would use its enigmatic weapon again, or whether the defenders realized that it was unnecessary.

About ten kilometers up, the screens of the *Eridanus* seemed to explode and she hung unprotected, a blunt torpedo of black metal, almost invisible against the sky. Instantly her light-absorbing paint, and the armor beneath, were torn off by the beams of the fortress. The great ship turned cherry-red, then white. She swung over so that her prow turned toward the Moon, and began her last dive. At first it seemed to Wheeler that she was heading straight toward him; then he saw that she was aimed at the fort. She was obeying her captain's last command.

It was almost a direct hit. The dying ship smashed into the lake of lava and exploded instantly, engulfing the fortress in an expanding hemisphere of flame. This, thought Wheeler, must surely be the end. He waited for the shock wave to reach him, and again watched the wall of dust sweep by—this time into the north. The concussion was so violent that it jerked him off his feet, and he did not see how anyone in the fort could have survived. Cautiously, he put down the mirror which had given him almost all his view of the battle, and peered over the edge of his trench. He did not know that the final paroxysm was yet to come.

Incredibly, the dome was still there, though now it seemed that part of it had been sheared away. And it was inert and life-less: its screens were down, its energies exhausted, its garrison, surely, already dead. If so, they had done their work. Of the remaining Federal ship, there was no sign. She was already retreating toward Mars, her main armament completely useless and her drive units on the point of failure. She would never fight again, yet in the few hours of life that were left to her, she had one more role to play.

"It's all over, Sid," Wheeler called into his suit radio. "It's safe to come and look now."

Jamieson climbed up out of a crack fifty meters away, holding the radiation detector in front of him.

"It's still hot around here," Wheeler heard him grumble, half to himself. "The sooner we get moving the better."

"Will it be safe to go back to Ferdinand and put through a radio——" began Wheeler. Then he stopped. Something was happening over by the dome.

In a blast like an erupting volcano, the ground tore apart. An enormous geyser began to soar into the sky, hurling great boulders thousands of meters toward the stars. It climbed swiftly above the plain, driving a thunderhead of smoke and spray before it. For a moment it towered against the southern sky, like some incredible, heaven-aspiring tree that had sprung from the barren soil of the Moon. Then, almost as swiftly as it had grown, it subsided in silent ruin and its angry vapors dispersed into space.

The thousands of tons of heavy liquid holding open the deepest shaft that man had ever bored had finally come to the boiling point, as the energies of the battle seeped into the rock. The mine had blown its top as spectacularly as any oil well on Earth, and had proved that an excellent explosion could still be arranged without the aid of atom bombs.

Chapter XVIII

TO THE OBSERVATORY, the battle was no more than an occasional distant earthquake, a faint vibration of the ground which disturbed some of the more delicate instruments but did no material damage. The psychological damage, however, was a different matter. Nothing is so demoralizing as to know that great and shattering events are taking place, but to be totally unaware of their outcome. The Observatory was full of wild rumors, the Signals Office besieged with inquiries. But even here there was no information. All news broadcasts from Earth had ceased; the whole world was waiting, as if with bated breath, for the fury of the battle to die away so that the victor could be known. That there would be no victor was the one thing that had not been anticipated.

Not until long after the last vibrations had died away and the radio had announced that the Federation forces were in full retreat did Maclaurin permit anyone to go up to the surface. The report that came down was, after the strain and excitement of the last few hours, not only a relief but a considerable anticlimax. There was a small amount of increased radioactivity about, but not the slightest trace of damage. What it would be like on the other side of the mountains was, of course, a different matter.

The news that Wheeler and Jamieson were safe gave a tremendous boost to the staff's morale. Owing to a partial breakdown of communications, it had taken them almost an hour to contact Earth and to get connected to the Observatory. The delay had been both infuriating and worrying, for it had left them wondering if the Observatory had been destroyed. They dared not set out on foot until they were sure they had somewhere to go—and Ferdinand was now too radioactive to be a safe refuge.

Sadler was in Communications trying to find out what was happening, when the message came through. Jamieson, sounding very tired, gave a brief report of the battle and asked for instructions.

"What's the radiation reading inside the cab?" Maclaurin asked. Jamieson called back the figures: it still seemed strange to Sadler that the message should have to go all the way to Earth just to span a hundred kilometers of the Moon, and he was never able to get used to the three-second delay that this implied.

"I'll get the health section to work out the tolerance," Maclaurin answered. "You say it's only a quarter of that reading out in the open?"

"Yes—we've stayed outside the tractor as much as possible, and have come in every ten minutes to try and contact you."

"The best plan is this—we'll send a Caterpillar right away, and you start walking toward us. Any particular rendezvous you'd like to aim for?"

Jamieson thought for a moment.

"Tell your driver to head for the five-kilometer marker on this side of Prospect; we'll reach it about the same time as he does. We'll keep our suit radios on so there'll be no chance of him missing us."

As Maclaurin was giving his orders, Sadler asked if there was room for an extra passenger in the rescue tractor. It would give him a chance of questioning Wheeler and Jamieson much sooner than would otherwise be the case. When they reached the Observatory—though they did not know it yet—they would be whipped into hospital at once and treated for radiation sickness.

129

They were in no serious danger, but Sadler doubted that he would have much chance of seeing them for a while when the doctors got hold of them.

Maclaurin granted the request, adding the comment: "Of course, you realize this means that you'll have to tell them who you are. Then the whole Observatory will know inside ten minutes."

"I've thought of that," Sadler replied. "It doesn't matter now." Always assuming, he added to himself, that it ever did.

Half an hour later, he was learning the difference between travel in the smooth, swift monorail and in a jolting tractor. After a while he became used to the nightmare grades the driver was light-heartedly attacking, and ceased to regret volunteering for this mission. Besides the operating crew, the vehicle was carrying the chief medical officer, who hoped to make blood counts and give injections as soon as the rescue had been effected.

There was no dramatic climax to the expedition; as soon as they topped Prospect Pass, they made radio contact with the two men trudging toward them. Fifteen minutes later the moving figures appeared on the skyline, and there was no ceremony apart from fervent handshakes as they came aboard the tractor.

They halted for a while so that the M.O. could give his injections and make his tests. When he had finished he told Wheeler: "You're going to be in bed for the next week, but there's no need to worry."

"What about me?" asked Jamieson.

"You're all right—a much smaller dose. A couple of days is all you need."

"It was worth it," said Wheeler cheerfully. "I don't think that was much of a price to pay for a grandstand view of Armageddon." Then, as the reaction of knowing that he was safe wore off, he added anxiously: "What's the latest news? Has the Federation attacked anywhere else?"

"No," Sadler replied. "It hasn't, and I doubt that it can. But it seems to have achieved its main objective, which was to stop us using that mine. What will happen now is up to the politicians."

"Hey," said Jamieson, "what are *you* doing here, anyway?"

Sadler smiled.

"I'm still investigating, but let's say that my terms of reference are wider than anyone imagined."

"You aren't a radio reporter?" asked Wheeler suspiciously.

"Er—not exactly. I'd rather not——"

"I know," Jamieson interjected suddenly. "You're something to do with Security. It makes sense now."

Sadler looked at him with mild annoyance. Jamieson, he decided, had a remarkable talent for making things difficult.

"It doesn't matter. But I want to send in a full report of everything you saw. You realize that you are the only surviving eyewitnesses, except for the crew of the Federal ship."

"I was afraid of that," said Jamieson. "So Project Thor was wiped out?"

"Yes, but I think it did its job."

"What a waste, though—Steffanson and all those others! If it hadn't been for me, he'd probably still be alive."

"He knew what he was doing—and he made his own choice," replied Sadler, rather curtly. Yes, Jamieson was going to be a most recalcitrant hero.

For the next thirty minutes, as they were climbing back over the wall of Plato on the homeward run, he questioned Wheeler about the course of the battle. Although the astronomer could only have seen a small part of the engagement, owing to his limited angle of view, his information would be invaluable when the tacticians back on Earth carried out their post-mortem.

"What puzzles me most of all," Wheeler concluded, "is the weapon the fort used to destroy the battleship. It looked like a beam of some kind, but of course that's impossible. *No* beam can be visible in a vacuum. And I wonder why they only used it once? Do *you* know anything about it?"

"I'm afraid not," replied Sadler, which was quite untrue. He still knew very little about the weapons in the fort, but this was the only one he now fully understood. He could well appreciate why a jet of molten metal, hurled through space at several hundred kilometers a second by the most powerful electromagnets ever built, might have looked like a beam of light flashing on for an instant. And he knew that it was a short-range weapon, designed to pierce the fields which would deflect ordinary pro-

131

jectiles. It could be used only under ideal conditions, and it took many minutes to recharge the gigantic condensers which powered the magnets.

This was a mystery the astonomers would have to solve for themselves. He did not imagine that it would take them very long, when they really turned their minds to the subject.

The tractor came crawling cautiously down the steep inner slopes of the great walled-plain, and the latticework of the telescopes appeared on the horizon. They looked, Sadler thought, exactly like a couple of factory chimneys surrounded by scaffolding. Even in his short stay here, he had grown quite fond of them and had come to think of them as personalities, just as did the men who used them. He could share the astronomer's concern that any harm might befall these superb instruments, which had brought knowledge back to Earth from a hundred thousand million light-years away in space.

A towering cliff cut them off from the sun, and darkness fell abruptly as they rolled into shadow. Overhead, the stars began to reappear as Sadler's eyes automatically adjusted for the change in light. He stared up into the northern sky, and saw that Wheeler was doing the same.

Nova Draconis was still among the brightest stars in the sky, but it was fading fast. In a few days, it would be no more brilliant than Sirius; in a few months, it would be beyond the grasp of the unaided eye. There was, surely, some message here, some symbol half glimpsed on the frontiers of imagination. Science would learn much from *N. Draconis,* but what would it teach the ordinary world of men?

Only this, thought Sadler. The heavens might blaze with portents, the galaxy might burn with the beacon lights of detonating stars, but man would go about his own affairs with a sublime indifference. He was busy with the planets now, and the stars would have to wait. He would not be overawed by anything that they could do; and in his own good time, he would deal with them as he considered fit.

Neither rescued nor rescuers had much to say on the last lap of the homeward journey. Wheeler was obviously beginning to suffer from delayed shock, and his hands had developed a nervous tremble. Jamieson merely sat and watched the Observatory

132

approaching, as if he had never seen it before. When they drove through the long shadow of the thousand-centimeter telescope, he turned to Sadler and asked: "Did they get everything under cover in time?"

"I believe so," Sadler replied. "I've not heard of any damage."

Jamieson nodded absent-mindedly. He showed no sign of pleasure or relief; he had reached emotional saturation, and nothing could really affect him now until the impact of the last few hours had worn away.

Sadler left them as soon as the tractor drove into the underground garage, and hurried to his room to write up his report. This was outside his terms of reference, but he felt glad that at least he was able to do something constructive.

There was a sense of anticlimax now—a feeling that the storm had spent its fury and would not return. In the aftermath of the battle, Sadler felt far less depressed than he had for days. It seemed to him that both Earth and the Federation must be equally overawed by the forces they had released, and both equally anxious for peace.

For the first time since he had left Earth, he dared to think once more of his future. Though it could still not be wholly dismissed, the danger of a raid on Earth itself now seemed remote. Jeannette was safe, and soon he might be seeing her again. At least he could tell her where he was, since events had made any further secrecy absurd.

But there was just one nagging frustration in Sadler's mind. He hated to leave a job undone, yet in the nature of things this mission of his might remain forever uncompleted. He would have given so much to have known whether or not there had been a spy in the Observatory.

Chapter XIX

THE LINER *Pegasus*, with three hundred passengers and a crew of sixty, was only four days out from Earth when the war began and ended. For some hours there had been a great confusion and alarm on board, as the radio messages from Earth and Federation were intercepted. Captain Halstead had been forced to take firm measures with some of the passengers, who wished to turn back rather than go on to Mars and an uncertain future as prisoners of war. It was not easy to blame them; Earth was still so close that it was a beautiful silver crescent, with the Moon a fainter and smaller echo beside it. Even from here, more than a million kilometers away, the energies that had just flamed across the face of the Moon had been clearly visible, and had done little to restore the morale of the passengers.

They could not understand that the law of celestial mechanics admit of no appeal. The *Pegasus* was barely clear of Earth, and still weeks from her intended goal. But she had reached her orbiting speed, and had launched herself like a giant projectile on the path that would lead inevitably to Mars, under the guidance of the sun's all-pervading gravity. There could be no turning back: that would be a maneuver involving an impossible amount of propellant. The *Pegasus* carried enough dust in her tanks to match velocity with Mars at the end of her orbit, and to allow for reasonable course corrections en route. Her nuclear reactors could provide energy for a dozen voyages—but sheer energy was useless if there was no propellant mass to eject. Whether she wanted to or not, the *Pegasus* was headed for Mars with the inevitability of a runaway streetcar. Captain Halstead did not anticipate a pleasant trip.

The words MAYDAY, MAYDAY came crashing out of the radio and banished all other preoccupations of the *Pegasus* and her crew. For three hundred years, in air and sea and space, these words had alerted rescue organizations, had made captains change their course and race to the aid of stricken comrades. But there was so little that the commander of a spaceship could do; in the whole history of astronautics, there have been only three cases of a successful rescue operation in space.

There are two main reasons for this, only one of which is widely advertised by the shipping lines. Any serious disaster in space is extremely rare; almost all accidents occur during planetfall or departure. Once a ship has reached space, and has swung into the orbit that will lead it effortlessly to its destination, it is safe from all hazards except internal, mechanical troubles. Such troubles occur more often than the passengers ever know, but are usually trivial and are quietly dealt with by the crew. All spaceships, by law, are built in several independent sections, any one of which can serve as a refuge in an emergency. So the worst that ever happens is that some uncomfortable hours are spent by all while an irate captain breathes heavily down the neck of his engineering officer.

The second reason why space rescues are so rare is that they are almost impossible, from the nature of things. Spaceships travel at enormous velocities on exactly calculated paths, which do not permit of major alterations—as the passengers of the *Pegasus* were now beginning to appreciate. The orbit any ship follows from one planet to another is unique; no other vessel will ever follow the same path again, among the changing patterns of the planets. There are no "shipping lanes" in space, and it is rare indeed for one ship to pass within a million kilometers of another. Even when this does happen, the difference of speed is almost always so great that contact is impossible.

All these thoughts flashed through Captain Halstead's mind when the message came down to him from Signals. He read the position and course of the distressed ship—the velocity figure must have been garbled in transmission, it was so ridiculously high. Almost certainly, there was nothing he could do— they were too far away, and it would take days to reach them.

Then he noticed the name at the end of the message. He thought he was familiar with every ship in space, but this was a new one to him. He stared in bewilderment for a moment before he suddenly realized just who was calling for his assistance. . . .

Enmity vanishes when men are in peril on sea or in space. Captain Halstead leaned over his control desk and said: "Signals! Get me their captain."

"He's on circuit, sir. You can go ahead."

Captain Halstead cleared his throat. This was a novel experience, and not a pleasant one. It gave him no sort of satisfaction to tell even an enemy that he could do nothing to save him.

"Captain Halstead, *Pegasus*, speaking," he began. "You're

135

too far away for contact. Our operational reserve is less than ten kilometers a second. I've no need to compute, I can see it's impossible. Have you any suggestions? Please confirm your velocity; we were given an incorrect figure."

The reply, after a four-second time-lag that seemed doubly maddening in these circumstances, was unexpected and astonishing.

"Commodore Brennan, Federal cruiser *Acheron*. I can confirm our velocity figure. We can contact you in two hours, and will make all course corrections ourselves. We still have power, but must abandon ship in less than three hours. Our radiation shielding has gone, and the main reactor is becoming unstable. We've got manual control on it, and it will be safe for at least an hour after we reach you. But we can't guarantee it beyond then."

Captain Halstead felt the scalp crawl at the back of his neck. He did not know how a reactor could became unstable, but he knew what would happen if one did. There were a good many things about the *Acheron* he did not understand—her speed, above all—but there was one point that emerged very clearly and upon which Commodore Brennan must be left in no doubt.

"*Pegasus* to *Acheron*," he replied. "I have three hundred passengers aboard. I cannot hazard my ship if there is danger of an explosion."

"There is no danger, I can guarantee that. We will have at least five minutes' warning, which will give us ample time to get clear of you."

"Very well—I'll get my airlocks ready and my crew standing by to pass you a line."

There was a pause longer than that dictated by the sluggish progress of radio waves. Then Brennan replied:

"That's our trouble. We're cut off in the forward section. There are no external locks here, and we have only five suits among a hundred and twenty men."

Halstead whistled and turned to his navigating officer before answering.

"There's nothing we can do for them," he said. "They'll have to crack the hull to get out, and that will be the end of everyone except the five men in the suits. We can't even lend them our own suits—there'll be no way we can get them aboard without letting down the pressure." He flicked over the microphone switch.

"*Pegasus* to *Acheron*. How do you suggest we can assist you?"

It was eerie to be speaking to a man who was already as good as dead. The traditions of space were as strict as those of the sea. Five men could leave the *Acheron* alive, but her captain would not be among them.

Halstead did not know that Commodore Brennan had other ideas, and had by no means abandoned hope, desperate though the situation on board the *Acheron* seemed. His chief medical officer, who had proposed the plan, was already explaining it to the crew.

"This is what we're going to do," said the small, dark man who a few months ago had been one of the best surgeons on Venus. "We can't get at the airlocks, because there's vacuum all round us and we've only got five suits. This ship was built for fighting, not for carrying passengers, and I'm afraid her designers had other matters to think about besides Standard Space-worthiness Regs. Here we are, and we have to make the best of it.

"We'll be alongside the *Pegasus* in a couple of hours. Luckily for us, she's got big locks for loading freight and passengers; there's room for thirty or forty men to crowd into them, if they squeeze tight—*and aren't wearing suits*. Yes, I know that sounds bad, but it's not suicide. You're going to breathe space, and get away with it! I won't say it will be enjoyable, but it will be something to brag about for the rest of your lives.

"Now listen carefully. The first thing I've got to prove to you is that you can live for five minutes without breathing—in fact, *without wanting to breathe*. It's a simple trick: Yogis and magicians have known it for centuries, but there's nothing occult about it and it's based on common-sense physiology. To give you confidence, I want you to make this test."

The M.O. pulled a stop watch out of his pocket, and continued:

"When I say 'Now!' I want you to exhale completely—empty your lungs of every drop of air—and then see how long you can stay before you have to take a breath. Don't strain—

just hold out until it becomes uncomfortable, then start breathing again normally. I'll start counting the seconds after fifteen, so you can tell what you managed to do. If anyone can't take the quarter minute, I'll recommend his instant dismissal from the Service."

The ripple of laughter broke the tension, as it had been intended to; then the M.O. held up his hand, and swept it down with a shout of "Now!" There was a great sigh as the entire company emptied its lungs; then utter silence.

When the M.O. started counting at "Fifteen," there were a few gasps from those who had barely been able to make the grade. He went on counting to "Sixty" accompanied by occasional explosive pants as one man after another capitulated. Some were still stubbornly holding out after a full minute.

"That's enough," said the little surgeon. "You tough guys can stop showing off, you're spoiling the experiment."

Again there was a murmur of amusement; the men were rapidly regaining their morale. They still did not understand what was happening, but at least some plan was afoot that offered them a hope of rescue.

"Let's see how we managed," said the M.O. "Hands up all those who held out for fifteen to twenty seconds. . . . Now twenty to twenty-five. . . . Now twenty-five to thirty—Jones, you're a damn liar—you folded up at fifteen! . . . Now thirty to thirty-five. . . ."

When he had finished the census, it was clear that more than half the company had managed to hold their breath for thirty seconds, and no one had failed to reach fifteen seconds.

"That's about what I expected," said the M.O. "You can regard this as a control experiment, and now we come on to the real thing. I ought to tell you that we're now breathing almost pure oxygen here, at about three hundred millimeters. So although the pressure in the ship is less than half its sea-level value on Earth, your lungs are taking in twice as much oxygen as they would on Earth, and still more than they would on Mars or Venus. If any of you have sneaked off to have a surreptitious smoke in the toilet, you'll already have noticed that the air was rich, as your cigarette will only have lasted a few seconds.

"I'm telling you all this because it will increase your confidence to know what is going on. What you're going to do now is to flush out your lungs and fill your system with oxygen. It's called hyperventilation, which is simply a ten dollar word for deep breathing. When I give the signal, I want you all to breathe as *deeply* as you can, then exhale *completely*, and carry on breathing in the same way until I tell you to stop. I'll let you do it for a minute; some of you may feel a bit dizzy at the end of that time, but it'll pass. Take in all the air you can with every breath; swing your arms to get maximum chest expansion.

"Then, when the minute's up, I'll tell you to exhale, then stop breathing, and I'll begin counting seconds again. I think I can promise you a big surprise. O.K.—here we go!"

For the next minutes, the overcrowded compartments of the *Acheron* presented a fantastic spectacle. More than a hundred men were flailing their arms and breathing stertorously, as if each was at his last gasp. Some were too closely packed together to breathe as deeply as they would have liked, and all had to anchor themselves somehow so that their exertion would not cause them to drift around the cabins.

"Now!" shouted the M.O. "Stop breathing—blow out all your air—and see how long you can manage before you've got to start again. I'll count the seconds, but this time I won't begin until half a minute has gone."

The result, it was obvious, left everyone flabbergasted. One man failed to make the minute, otherwise almost two minutes elapsed before most of the men felt the need to breathe again. Indeed, to have taken a breath before then would have demanded a deliberate effort. Some men were still perfectly comfortable after three or four minutes; one was holding out at five when the doctor stopped him.

"I think you'll all see what I was trying to prove. When your lungs are flushed out with oxygen, you just don't *want* to breathe for several minutes, any more than you want to eat again after a heavy meal. It's no strain or hardship; it's not a question of holding your breath. And if your life depended on it, you could do even better than this, I promise you.

"Now we're going to tie up right alongside the *Pegasus;* it will take less than thirty seconds to get over to her. She'll have

139

her men out in suits to push along any stragglers, and the air lock doors will be slammed shut as soon as you're all inside. Then the lock will be flooded with air and you'll be none the worse except for some bleeding noses."

He hoped that was true. There was only one way to find out. It was a dangerous and unprecedented gamble, but there was no alternative. At least it would give every man a fighting chance for his life.

"Now," he continued, "you're probably wondering about the pressure drop. That's the only uncomfortable part, but you won't be in a vacuum long enough for severe damage. We'll open the hatches in two stages; first we'll drop pressure slowly to a tenth of an atmosphere, then we'll blow out completely in one bang and make a dash for it. Total decompression's painful, but not dangerous. Forget all that nonsense you may have heard about the human body blowing up in a vacuum. We're a lot tougher than that, and the final drop we're going to make from a tenth of an atmosphere to zero is considerably less than men have already stood in lab tests. Hold your mouth wide open and let yourself break wind. You'll feel your skin stinging all over, but you'll probably be too busy to notice that."

The M.O. paused, and surveyed his quiet, intent audience. They were all taking it very well, but that was only to be expected. Every one was a trained man—they were the pick of the planets' engineers and technicians.

"As a matter of fact," the surgeon continued cheerfully, "you'll probably laugh when I tell you the biggest danger of the lot. It's nothing more than sunburn. Out there you'll be in the sun's raw ultra-violet, unshielded by atmosphere. It can give you a nasty blister in thirty seconds, so we'll make the crossing in the shadow of the *Pegasus*. If you happen to get outside that shadow, just shield your face with your arm. Those of you who've got gloves might as well wear them.

"Well, that's the picture. I'm going to cross with the first team just to show how easy it is. Now I want you to split up into four groups, and I'll drill you each separately."

Side by side, the *Pegasus* and the *Acheron* raced toward the distant planet that only one of them would ever reach. The

140

airlocks of the liner were open, gaping wide no more than a few meters from the hull of the crippled battleship. The space between the two vessels was strung with guide ropes, and among them floated the men of the liner's crew, ready to give assistance if any of the escaping men were overcome during the brief but dangerous crossing.

It was lucky for the crew of the *Acheron* that four pressure bulkheads were still intact. Their ship could still be divided into four separate compartments, so that a quarter of the crew could leave at a time. The airlocks of the *Pegasus* could not have held everyone at once if a mass escape had been necessary.

Captain Halstead watched from the bridge as the signal was given. There was a sudden puff of smoke from the hull of the battleship, then the emergency hatch—certainly never designed for an emergency such as *this*—blew away into space. A cloud of dust and condensing vapor blasted out, obscuring the view for a second. He knew how the waiting men would feel the escaping air sucking at their bodies, trying to tear them away from their handholds.

When the cloud had dispersed, the first men had already emerged. The leader was wearing a spacesuit, and all the others were strung on the three lines attached to him. Instantly, men from the *Pegasus* grabbed two of the lines and darted off to their respective airlocks. The men of the *Acheron,* Halstead was relieved to see, all appeared to be conscious and to be doing everything they could to help.

It seemed ages before the last figure on its drifting line was towed or pushed into an airlock. Then the voice from one of those spacesuited figures out there shouted, "Close Number Three!" Number One followed almost at once; but there was an agonizing delay before the signal for Two came. Halstead could not see what was happening; presumably someone was still outside and holding up the rest. But at last all the locks were closed. There was no time to fill them in the normal way; the valves were jerked open by brute force and the chambers flooded with air from the ship.

Aboard the *Acheron*, Commodore Brennan waited with his remaining ninety men, in the three compartments that were still unsealed. They had formed their groups and were strung in chains of ten behind their leaders. Everything had been planned and rehearsed; the next few seconds would prove whether or not in vain.

Then the ship's speakers announced, in an almost quietly conversational tone:

"Pegasus to Acheron. We've got all your men out of the locks. No casualties. A few hemorrhages. Give us five minutes to get ready for the next batch."

They lost one man on the last transfer. He panicked and they had to slam the lock shut without him, rather than risk the lives of all the others. It seemed a pity that they could not all have made it, but for the moment everyone was too thankful to worry about that.

There was only one thing still to be done. Commodore Brennan, the last man aboard the *Acheron,* adjusted the timing circuit that would start the drive in thirty seconds. That would give him long enough; even in his clumsy spacesuit he could get out of the open hatch in half that time. It was cutting it fine, but only he and his engineering officer knew how narrow the margin was.

He threw the switch and dived for the hatch. He had already reached the *Pegasus* when the ship he had commanded, still loaded with millions of kilowatt-centuries of energy, came to life for the last time and dwindled silently toward the stars of the Milky Way.

The explosion was easily visible among all the inner planets. It blew to nothingness the last ambitions of the Federation, and the last fears of Earth.

Chapter XX

EVERY EVENING, as the sun drops down beyond the lonely pyramid of Pico, the shadow of the great mountain reaches out to engulf the metal column that will stand in the Sea of Rains as long as the Sea itself endures. There are five hundred and twenty-seven names on that column, in alphabetical order. No mark distinguishes the men who died for the Federation from those who died for Earth, and perhaps this simple fact is the best proof that they did not die in vain.

The Battle of Pico ended the domination of Earth and marked the coming of age of the planets. Earth was weary after her long saga and the efforts she had put forth to conquer the nearer worlds—those worlds which had now so inexplicably turned against her, as long ago the American colonies had turned against their motherland. In both cases the reasons were similar, and in both the eventual outcomes equally advantageous to mankind.

Had either side won a clearcut victory, it might have been a disaster. The Federation might have been tempted to impose on Earth an agreement which it could never enforce. Earth, on the other hand, might well have crippled its errant children by withdrawing all supplies, thus setting back for centuries the colonization of the planets.

Instead, it had been a stalemate. Each antagonist had learned a sharp and salutary lesson; above all, each had learned to respect the other. And each was now very busy explaining to its citizens exactly what it had been doing in their names. . . .

The last explosion of the war was followed, within a few hours, by political explosions on Earth, Mars and Venus. When the smoke had drifted away, many ambitious personalities had disappeared, at least for the time being, and those in power had one main objective—to re-establish friendly relations, and to erase the memory of an episode which did credit to no one.

The *Pegasus* incident, cutting across the divisions of war and reminding men of their essential unity, made the task of the statesmen far easier than it might otherwise have been. The Treaty of Phobos was signed in what one historian called an atmosphere of shamefaced conciliation. Agreement was swift, for Earth and Federation each possessed something that the other needed badly.

The superior science of the Federation had given it the secret of the accelerationless drive, as it is now universally but inaccurately called. For its part, Earth was now prepared to share the wealth she had tapped far down within the Moon. The barren crust had been penetrated, and at last the heavy core was yielding

143

up its stubbornly guarded treasures. There was wealth here that would supply all man's needs for centuries to come.

It was destined, in the years ahead, to transform the solar system and to alter completely the distribution of the human race. Its immediate effect was to make the Moon, long the poor relation of the old and wealthy Earth, into the richest and most important of all the worlds. Within ten years, the Independent Lunar Republic would be dictating F.O.B. terms to Earth and Federation with equal impartiality.

But the future would take care of itself. All that mattered now was that the war was over.

Chapter XXI

CENTRAL CITY, thought Sadler, had grown since he was here thirty years ago. Any one of these domes could cover the whole seven they had back in the old days. How long would it be, at this rate, before the whole Moon was covered up? He rather hoped it would not be in his time.

The station itself was almost as large as one of the old domes. Where there had been five tracks, there were now thirty. But the design of the monocabs had not altered much, and their speed seemed to be about the same. The vehicle which had brought him from the spaceport might well have been the one that had carried him across the Sea of Rains a quarter of a lifetime ago.

A quarter of a lifetime, that is, if you were a citizen of the Moon and could expect to see your one hundred and twentieth birthday. But a full third of a lifetime if you spent all your waking and sleeping hours fighting the gravity of Earth. . . .

There were far more vehicles in the streets; Central City was too big to operate on a pedestrian basis now. But one thing had not changed. Overhead was the blue, cloud-flecked sky of Earth, and Sadler did not doubt that the rain still came on schedule.

He jumped into an autocab and dialed the address, relaxing as he was carried through the busy streets. His baggage had already gone to the hotel, and he was in no hurry to follow it. As soon as he arrived there, business would catch up with him again, and he might not have another chance of carrying out this mission.

There seemed almost as many businessmen and tourists from Earth here as there were residents. It was easy to distinguish them, not only by their clothes and behavior but by the way they walked in this low gravity. Sadler was surprised to find that though he had been on the Moon only a few hours, the automatic muscular adjustment he had learned so long ago came smoothly into play again. It was like learning to ride a bicycle; once you had achieved it, you never forgot.

So they had a lake here now, complete with islands and swans. He had read about the swans; their wings had to be carefully clipped to prevent their flying away and smashing into the "sky." There was a sudden splash as a large fish broke the surface; Sadler wondered if it was surprised to find how high it could jump out of the water.

The cab, threading its way above the buried guide-rods, swooped down a tunnel that must lead beneath the edge of the dome. Because the illusion of sky was so well contrived, it was not easy to tell when you were about to leave one dome and enter another, but Sadler knew where he was when the vehicle went past the great metal doors at the lowest part of the tube. These doors, so he had been told, could smash shut in less than two seconds, and would do so automatically if there was a pressure drop on either side. Did such thoughts as these, he wondered, ever give sleepless nights to the inhabitants of Central City? He very much doubted it; a considerable fraction of the human race had spent its life in the shadow of volcanoes, dams and dykes, without developing any signs of nervous tension. Only once had one of the domes of Central City been evacuated —in both senses of the word—and that was due to a slow leak that had taken hours to be effective.

The cab rose out of the tunnel into the residential area, and Sadler was faced with a complete change of scenery. This was no dome encasing a small city; this was a single giant building in itself, with moving corridors instead of streets. The cab came to a halt, and reminded him in polite tones that it would wait thirty minutes for an extra one-fifty. Sadler, who thought it might take him that length of time even to find the place he was looking for, declined the offer and the cab pulled away in search of fresh customers.

There was a large bulletin board a few meters away, displaying a three-dimensional map of the building. The whole place reminded Sadler of a type of beehive used many centuries ago, which he had once seen illustrated in an old encyclopedia. No doubt it was absurdly easy to find your way around when you'd got used to it, but for the moment he was quite baffled by Floors, Corridors, Zones and Sectors.

"Going somewhere, mister?" said a small voice behind him.

Sadler turned round, and saw a boy of six or seven years looking at him with alert, intelligent eyes. He was just about the same age as Jonathan Peter II. Lord, it *had* been a long time since he last visited the Moon. . . .

"Don't often see Earth folk here," said the youngster. "You lost?"

"Not yet," Sadler replied. "But I suspect I soon will be."

"Where going?"

If there was a "you" in that sentence, Sadler missed it. It was really astonishing that, despite the interplanetary radio networks, distinct differences of speech were springing up on the various worlds. This boy could doubtless speak perfectly good Earth-English when he wanted to, but it was not his language of everyday communication.

Sadler looked at the rather complex address in his notebook, and read it out slowly.

"Come on," said his self-appointed guide. Sadler gladly obeyed.

The ramp ahead ended abruptly in a broad, slowly moving roller-road. This carried them forward a few meters, then decanted them on to a high-speed section. After sweeping at least a kilometer past the entrances to countless corridors, they were switched back on to a slow section and carried to a huge, hexagonal concourse. It was crowded with people, coming and going from one roadway to another, and pausing to make purchases at little kiosks. Rising through the center of the busy scene were two spiral ramps, one carrying the up and the other the down traffic. They stepped on to the "Up" spiral and let the moving surface lift them half a dozen floors. Standing at the edge of the ramp, Sadler could see that the building extended downward for an immense distance. A very long way below was something that looked like a large net. He did some mental calculations, then decided that it would, after all, be adequate to break the fall of anyone foolish enough to go over the edge. The architects of lunar buildings had a light-hearted approach to gravity which would lead to instant disaster on Earth.

The upper concourse was exactly like the one by which they had entered, but there were fewer people about and one could tell that, however democratic the Autonomous Lunar Republic might be, there were subtle class distinctions here as in all other cultures that man had ever created. There was no more aristocracy of birth or wealth, but that of responsibility would always exist. Here, no doubt, lived the people who really ran the Moon. They had few more possessions, and a good many more worries, than their fellow citizens on the floors below, and there was a continual interchange from one level to another.

Sadler's small guide led him out of this central concourse along yet another moving passageway, then finally into a quiet corridor with a narrow strip of garden down its center and a fountain playing at either end. He marched up to one of the doors and announced: "Here's place." The brusqueness of his statement was quite neutralized by the proud there-wasn't-that-clever-of-me smile he gave Sadler, who was now wondering what would be a suitable reward for his enterprise. Or would the boy be offended if he gave him anything?

This social dilemma was solved for him by his observant guide.

"More than ten floors, that's fifteen."

So there's a standard rate, thought Sadler. He handed over a quarter, and to his surprise was compelled to accept the change. He had not realized that the well-known lunar virtues of honesty, enterprise and fair-dealing started at such an early age.

"Don't go yet," he said to his guide as he rang the doorbell. "If there's no one in, I'll want you to take me back."

"You not phoned first?" said that practical person, looking at him incredulously.

Sadler felt it was useless to explain. The inefficiencies and vagaries of old-fashioned Earth-folk were not appreciated by

147

these energetic colonists—though heaven help him if he ever used *that* word here.

However, there was no need for the precaution. The man he wanted to meet was at home, and Sadler's guide waved him a cheerful good-by as he went off down the corridor, whistling a tune that had just arrived from Mars.

"I wonder if you remember me," said Sadler. "I was at the Plato Observatory during the Battle of Pico. My name's Bertram Sadler."

"Sadler? Sadler? Sorry, but I don't remember you at the moment. But come right in; I'm always pleased to meet old friends."

Sadler followed into the house, looking round curiously as he did so. It was the first time he had ever been into a private home on the Moon, and as he might have expected there was no way in which it could be distinguished from a similar residence on Earth. That it was one cell in a vast honeycomb did not make it any less a home; it had been two centuries since more than a minute fraction of the human race had lived in separate, isolated buildings and the word "house" had changed its meaning with the times.

There was just one touch in the main living room, however, that was too old-fashioned for any terrestrial family. Extending halfway across one wall was a large animated mural of a kind which Sadler had not seen for years. It showed a snow-flecked mountainside sloping down to a tiny Alpine village a kilometer or more below. Despite the apparent distance, every detail was crystal clear; the little houses and the toy church had the sharp, vivid distinctness of something seen through the wrong end of a telescope. Beyond the village, the ground rose again, more and more steeply, to the great mountain that dominated the skyline and trailed from its summit a perpetual plume of snow, a white streamer drifting forever down the wind.

It was, Sadler guessed, a real scene recorded a couple of centuries ago. But he could not be sure; Earth still had such surprises in out-of-the-way spots.

He took the seat he was offered and had his first good look at the man he had played truant from rather important business to meet. "You don't remember me?" he said.

"I'm afraid not—but I'm quite bad at names and faces."

"Well, I'm nearly twice as old now, so it's not surprising. But *you* haven't changed, Professor Molton. I can still remember that you were the first man I ever spoke to on my way to the Observatory. I was riding the monorail from Central City, watching the sun going down behind the Apennines. It was the night before the Battle of Pico, and my first visit to the Moon."

Sadler could see that Molton was genuinely baffled. It was thirty years, after all, and he must not forget that he had a completely abnormal memory for faces and facts.

"Never mind," he continued. "I couldn't really expect you to remember me, because I wasn't one of your colleagues. I was only a visitor to the Observatory, and I wasn't there long. I'm an accountant, not an astronomer."

"Indeed?" said Molton, clearly still at a loss.

"That was not, however, the capacity in which I visited the Observatory, though I pretended it was. At the time, I was actually a government agent investigating a security leak."

He was watching the old man's face intently, and there was no mistaking the flicker of surprise. After a short silence, Molton replied, "I seem to remember something of the kind. But I'd quite forgotten the name. It was such a long time ago, of course."

"Yes, of course," echoed Sadler. "But I'm sure there are some things you'll remember. However, before I go on, there's one thing I'd better make clear. My visit here is quite unofficial. I really *am* nothing but an accountant now, and I'm glad to say quite a successful one. In fact, I'm one of the partners of Carter, Hargreaves and Tillotson, and I'm here to audit a number of the big lunar corporations. Your Chamber of Commerce will confirm that."

"I don't quite see——" began Molton.

"——what it's all got to do with you? Well, let me jog your memory. I was sent to the Observatory to investigate a security leak. Somehow, information was getting to the Federation. One of our agents had reported that the leak was at the Observatory, and I went there to look for it."

"Go on," said Molton.

Sadler smiled, a little wryly.

149

"I'm considered to be a good accountant," he said, "but I'm afraid I was not a very successful security man. I suspected a lot of people, but found nothing, though I accidentally uncovered one crook."

"Jenkins," said Molton suddenly.

"That's right—your memory's not so bad, Professor. Anyway, I never found the spy; I couldn't even prove that he existed, though I investigated every possibility I could think of. The whole affair fizzled out eventually, of course, and a few months later I was back at my normal work, and much happier too. But it has always worried me; it was a loose end I didn't like having round—a discrepancy in the balance sheet. I'd given up any hope of settling it, until a couple of weeks ago. Then I read Commodore Brennan's book. Have you seen it yet?"

"I'm afraid not, though of course I've heard about it."

Sadler reached into his briefcase and produced a fat volume, which he handed over to Molton.

"I've brought a copy for you—I know you'll be *very* interested. It's quite a sensational book, as you can judge by the fuss it's causing all over the System. He doesn't pull any punches, and I can understand why a lot of people in the Federation are pretty mad with him. However, that's not the point that concerns me. What I found quite fascinating was his account of the events leading up to the Battle of Pico. Imagine my surprise when he definitely confirmed that vital information had come from the Observatory. To quote his phrase: 'One of Earth's leading astronomers, by a brilliant technical subterfuge, kept us informed of developments during the progress of Project Thor. It would be improper to give his name, but he is now living in honored retirement on the Moon.'"

There was a very long pause. Molton's craggy face had now set in granite folds, and gave no hint of his emotions.

"Professor Molton," Sadler continued earnestly. "I hope you'll believe me when I say that I'm here purely out of private curiosity. In any case, you're a citizen of the Republic—there's nothing I could do to you even if I wanted to. *But I know you were that agent.* The description fits, and I've ruled out all the other possibilities. Moreover, some friends of mine in the Federation have been looking at records, again quite unofficially.

150

It's not the slightest use pretending you know nothing about it. If you don't want to talk, I'll clear out. But if you feel like telling me—and I don't see how it matters now—I'd give a very great deal to know how you managed to do it."

Molton had opened Professor, late Commodore, Brennan's book and was leafing through the index. Then he shook his head in some annoyance.

"He shouldn't have said that," he remarked testily, to no one in particular. Sadler breathed a sigh of satisfied anticipation. Abruptly, the old scientist turned upon him.

"If I tell you, what use will you make of the information?"

"None, I swear."

"Some of my colleagues might be annoyed, even after this time. It wasn't easy, you know. I didn't enjoy it either. But Earth had to be stopped, and I think I did the right thing."

"Professor Jamieson—he's director now, isn't he?—had similar ideas. But he didn't put them into practice."

"I know. There was a time when I nearly confided in him, but perhaps it's just as well that I didn't."

Molton paused reflectively, and his face creased into a smile.

"I've just remembered," he said. "I showed you round my lab. I was a little bit suspicious then—I thought it odd you should have come when you did. So I showed you *absolutely everything*, until I could see you were bored and had had enough."

"That happened rather often," said Sadler dryly. "There was quite a lot of equipment at the Observatory."

"Some of mine, however, was unique. Not even a man in my own field would have guessed what it did. I suppose your people were looking for concealed radio transmitters, and that sort of thing?"

"Yes; we had monitors on the lookout, but they never spotted anything."

Molton was obviously beginning to enjoy himself. Perhaps he too, thought Sadler, had been frustrated for the last thirty years, unable to say how he had fooled the security forces of Earth.

"The beauty of it was," Molten continued, "my transmitter was in full sight all the time. In fact, it was about the most

151

obvious thing in the Observatory. You see, it was the thousand-centimeter telescope."

Sadler stared at him incredulously.

"I don't understand you."

"Consider," said Molton, becoming once more the college professor he had been after leaving the Observatory, "exactly what it is a telescope does. It gathers light from a tiny portion of the sky, and brings it accurately to a focus on a photographic plate or the slit of a spectroscope. But don't you see—*a telescope can work both ways.*"

"I'm beginning to follow."

"My observing program involved using the thousand centimeter for studying faint stars. I worked in the far ultra-violet —which of course is quite invisible to the eye. I'd only to replace my usual instruments by an ultra-violet lamp, and the telescope immediately became a searchlight of immense power and accuracy, sending out a beam so narrow that it could only be detected in the exact portion of the sky I'd aimed it at. Interrupting the beam for signaling purposes was, of course, a trivial problem. I can't send Morse, but I built an automatic modulator to do it for me."

Sadler slowly absorbed this revelation. Once explained, the idea was ridiculously simple. Yes, any telescope, now he came to think of it, *must* be capable of working both ways—of gathering light from the stars, or of sending an almost perfectly parallel beam back at them, if one shone a light into the eyepiece end. Molton had turned the thousand-centimeter reflector into the largest electric torch ever built.

"Where did you aim your signals?" he asked.

"The Federation had a small ship about ten million kilometers out. Even at that distance, my beam was still pretty narrow and it needed good navigation to keep in it. The arrangement was that the ship would always keep dead in line between me and a faint northern star that was always visible above my horizon. When I wanted to send a signal—they knew when I would be operating, of course—I merely had to feed the co-ordinates into the telescope, and I'd be sure that they'd receive me. They had a small telescope aboard, with an ultra-violet detector. They kept in contact with Mars by ordinary radio. I often thought it must have been very dull out there, just listening for me. Sometimes I didn't send anything for days."

"That's another point," Sadler remarked. "How did the information get to *you*, anyway?"

"Oh, there were two methods. We got copies of all the astronomical journals, of course. There were agreed pages in certain journals—*The Observatory*, I recall, was one of them—that I kept my eye on. Some of the letters were fluorescent under far ultra-violet. No one could have spotted it; ordinary u.v. was no use."

"And the other method?"

"I used to go to the gym in Central City every weekend. You leave your clothes in locked cubicles when you undress, but there's enough clearance at the top of the doors for anything to be slipped in. Sometimes I used to find an ordinary tabulating-machine card on top of my things, with a set of holes punched in it. Perfectly commonplace and innocent, of course—you'll find them all over the Observatory, and not only in the Computing section. I always made a point of having a few genuine ones in my pockets. When I got back, I'd decipher the card and send the message out on my next transmission. I never knew what I was sending—it was always in code. And I never discovered who dropped the cards in my locker."

Molton paused, and looked quizzically at Sadler.

"On the whole," he concluded, "I really don't think you had much chance. My only danger was that you might catch my contacts and find they were passing information to me. Even if that happened, I thought I could get away with it. Every piece of apparatus I used had some perfectly genuine astronomical function. Even the modulator was part of an unsuccessful spectrum analyzer I'd never bothered to dismantle. And my transmissions only lasted for a few minutes; I could send a lot in that time, and then get on with my regular program."

Sadler looked at the old astronomer with undisguised admiration. He was beginning to feel a good deal better: an ancient inferiority complex had been exorcised. There was no need for self-reproach; he doubted if anyone could have detected Molton's activities, while they were confined to the

153

Observatory end alone. The people to blame were the counter-agents in Central City and Project Thor, who should have stopped the leak further up the line.

There was still one question that Sadler wished to ask, but could not bring himself to do so; it was, after all, no real concern of his. *How* was no longer a mystery; *why* still remained.

He could think of many answers. His studies of the past had shown him that a man like Molton would not become a spy for money, or power, or any such trivial reason. Some emotional impulse must have driven him on the path he followed, and he would have acted from a profound inner conviction that what he did was right. Logic might have told him that the Federation should be supported against Earth, but in a case like this, logic was never enough.

Here was one secret that would remain with Molton. Perhaps he was aware of Sadler's thoughts, for abruptly he walked over to the wide bookcase and slid aside a section of the paneling.

"I came across a quotation once," he said, "that's been a considerable comfort to me. I'm not sure whether it was supposed to be cynical or not, but there's a great deal of truth in it. It was made, I believe, by a French statesman named Talleyrand, about four hundred years ago. And he said this: *'What is treason? Merely a matter of dates.'* You might care to think that over, Mr. Sadler."

He walked back from the bookcase, carrying two glasses and a large decanter.

"A hobby of mine," he informed Sadler. "The last vintage from Hesperus. The French make fun of it, but I'd match it against anything from Earth."

They touched glasses.

"To peace among the planets," said Professor Molton, "and may no men ever again have to play the parts we did."

Against a landscape four hundred thousand kilometers away in space and two centuries ago in time, spy and counterspy drank the toast together. Each was full of memories, but those memories held no bitterness now. There was nothing more to say: for both of them, the story was ended.

Molton took Sadler down the corridor, past the quiet fountains, and saw him safely on the rolling floor that led to the main concourse. As he walked back to the house, lingering by the fragrant little garden, he was almost bowled over by a troop of laughing children racing across to the playground in Sector Nine. The corridor echoed briefly with their shrill voices; then they were gone like a sudden gust of wind.

Professor Molton smiled as he watched them racing toward their bright, untroubled future—the future he had helped to make. He had many consolations, and that was the greatest of them. Never again, as far ahead as imagination could roam, would the human race be divided against itself. For above him beyond the roof of Central City, the inexhaustible wealth of the Moon was flowing outward across space, to all the planets Man now called his own.